ABOUT THE AUTHOR

Because **Charlie Cochrane** couldn't be trusted to do any of her jobs of choice—like managing a rugby team—she writes. Her mystery novels include the Edwardian era *Cambridge Fellows* series, and the contemporary *Lindenshaw Mysteries*. Multi-published, she has titles with Carina, Riptide, Endeavour and Bold Strokes, among others.

A member of the Romantic Novelists' Association, Mystery People and International Thriller Writers Inc, Charlie regularly appears at literary festivals and at reader and author conferences with The Deadly Dames.

ISBN 9781912582174

Williams & Whiting (Publishers)

15 Chestnut Grove, Hurstpierpoint,

West Sussex, BN6 9SS

Pack Up Your
TROUBLES

Charlie Cochrane

Williams and Whiting

THIS GROUND WHICH WAS SECURED AT GREAT EXPENSE

August 1914, London

War and rumours of war.

They'd spoken of it for long enough in the smoking room at Warne's, of the great powder keg of Europe waiting for a single spark to ignite it. Now the explosion would rock the whole world.

Nicholas Southwell stared at people scurrying through the foyer like garden ants thrown into panic by the autumnal arrival of the flying variety, spreading the news of an impending attack. So it had come to war at last. All the club was buzzing with the news, the usual calm, archaic atmosphere shattered. Even men who were already old when the Boer War, that last great disturbance for the members, had erupted were speaking in vigorous tones of offering their strength, brains and energy to King George.

Nicholas had plenty of all three commodities—and business acumen, although he wasn't sure how that could be employed to serve his country. When his father had died, leaving him to inherit, the estate had been sound though small; he'd maintained the success of the business ventures, preserved and enlarged all that was good. They brought in a steady income and gave him a solid roof over his head, which was more than could be said for some of his neighbours for whom the twentieth century had brought little but debts and leaking tiles.

"Dam's burst at last, eh, Southwell?" Lord Spreadbury eased himself into the leather chair in Nicholas's preferred corner of the reading room, a place most favoured by those who kept themselves to themselves.

"So it appears." Nicholas laid down his newspaper, recognising he'd get no more peace or quiet today. "And whether all Europe will be flooded remains to be seen."

"It'll be over in a twelvemonth." Spreadbury waved his arm in a dismissive gesture. "Our boys will teach the Germans a thing or two, then march home victorious. Johnny Foreigner will never be a match for the British bulldog."

"Will you sign up, my lord?" Nicholas caught the quickly hidden look of some dark emotion—discomfort or fear—on the other man's face and knew his barb had struck home.

"I don't think they'd want old men like me getting in the way. I'll leave it to you youngsters to have your hour of glory this time around." Spreadbury rose. "I'll get myself an *Evening Standard* and see if the appeasers are spouting any nonsense."

Nicholas watched his retreating figure; Lord Spreadbury, at a guess, was barely forty—five and still in his prime. *Coward.* One of the few things he could recall his mother telling him as a child were stories about cowards, how *they always came to a bad end unless they saw the errors of their ways, Nicholas*. If she'd been alive now, Lady Southwell would have been the first to lead the local recruitment drive, using her charms to persuade young men to sign up.

I should go and get the Evening Standard *as well*. It was doubtful the newspaper would be any more accurate than the buzz of rumour was, but Nicholas wanted to know what people were being told.

He caught his reflection in the long mirror by the porters' desk, then stood transfixed, as if seeing himself clearly for the first time. He saw his mother's grey eyes and elegant nose, yet the Southwell stamp was on him in the dark hair and determined chin. An only child, his visage bore the sole living likeness of his parents and the possibility of having his own child to inherit the distinctive Southwell jaw seemed extremely remote. *Who'll miss you if you march away with the rest of them? Will there be a Nicholas Southwell—shaped fissure in anyone's life? In anyone's heart?*

Poor Mama; a teary goodbye on a platform in London or the dock at Southampton would have finished her, even if the tumour hadn't. She'd never been the same since Sir Robert, Nicholas's father, had died, victim to a catastrophic fall from his hunter just a year after the old queen passed on. Lady Southwell hadn't let Nicholas ride after that, not even exercising one of the mares along the wide, safe paddock by the river. She would never have coped with him volunteering to serve his country, no matter how keen she would have been for other people's sons to go.

Lady Southwell looked out from his reflection's eyes, pleading with him. *Wait and see, Nicholas. Bide your time.*

His father spoke from the clean cut jawline. *Do your duty, old man. No one to grieve for you now my lovely girl's gone.*

3

Nicholas sighed; maybe he was lucky to have the debate going on only in his head rather than over his dinner table. Perhaps it was as well not to leave anyone behind to grieve. There was Nanny, of course—she'd sniffle into her handkerchief but she'd keep calling him brave and noble, making him feel less like some officer in khaki than a knight in shining armour from one of the stories she used to read when he was no more than a boy.

He would have to write to her; she'd expect that. Maybe she'd even share his letters with the rest of the staff—they'd be keen to have news of how their master was getting on. He'd write to Haskell as well; Nicholas wouldn't need to keep half an eye out of the battlefield and onto estate business if Haskell was there to manage it in his absence. All would be safe on the home front.

Paul Haskell. His father had run the estate and related business for Sir Robert, and Paul had inherited the job two years after Nicholas had inherited the property. He was all that an employer could ask for: meticulous, honest, hard—working. And as handsome as Adonis. Nicholas closed his eyes, remembering Paul Haskell playing tennis on the lawn at the back of the house at one of Lady Southwell's many house parties—she'd loved entertaining, especially when she could fill the house with pretty girls she hoped would catch her son's eye.

She hadn't succeeded. Nicholas had refused to be regarded as breeding stock, some stallion that could be put to the mare, and it had almost brought him to blows with Sir Robert. From the day he turned eighteen, his

4

father had insisted that he settle down, preserve the family name, and secure the inheritance. No one could force him into the livestock ring now.

The image in the mirror seemed to dissolve into green and white. Paul Haskell stooping to lob the ball, immaculate white flannels clinging to his wiry frame. Nicholas could imagine the scene vividly, could hear the sound of ball on racket, could smell buddleia and girls' scent. While there were plenty of eligible young men to be had in the county, few played tennis as well as Haskell, nor were they as handsome. Green eyes framed by a clear—skinned face which saw plenty of fresh air, and topped by a mass of black locks—Haskell's colouration was unusual and his fine frame lacked nothing a girl could require to sigh over. There used to be an awful lot of sighing at Lady Southwell's parties.

Nicholas was certain that none of the fillies who'd been paraded for *his* perusal and who'd all received the same polite indifference had been served by the stallion who strode the tennis lawn. Nice girls didn't generally do such things outside the lawful marriage bed, or so he'd been led to believe. He couldn't say the same for the nursery maids or governesses he sometimes spied clinging to Paul's arm after church; their reputation wasn't quite so immaculate. He'd never asked, and Paul had never ventured to tell him, whether there was some girl he had his eye on, someone whom Nicholas would find with a toddler at her heels, a baby in a pram and Paul's ring on her finger when he came back from France.

Assuming Paul stayed at home for the war. What if he signed up?

A wave of panic crept up Nicholas' spine. Paul was plenty young enough, just past his thirtieth birthday—Nicholas had given him a hunter watch to mark the occasion, to replace one he'd broken taking a tumble down the stairs from the bell tower at St. Mary's. Paul had said he'd repay the compliment when Nicholas turned the same age in 1916, but would either of them see that date?

Nicholas' alarm subsided as he remembered why the fall had been so bad. *Congenital weakness in the right leg. Doesn't bother me usually but sometimes it just seems to cave in and I go arse over tip like a drunken sailor.* They'd never let him serve if he was half—crippled; he'd be safe at home. Nicholas wouldn't feel he had returned home until he saw Paul's smile.

Dear God, he would miss him.

"Are you feeling quite all right, sir?" The porter's voice bore the proper level of objective concern.

Nicholas realised he'd been standing too long in front of the mirror, deep in thought and memory. He glanced around, dreading the sight of some old buffer watching him, but only the porter seemed to have noticed his reverie. "I'm fine, thank you. Just thinking—these times give us all pause for thought."

"Indeed, sir." The porter bowed then returned to his desk, suitably chastened, as Nicholas strode purposefully towards the door.

He took a deep breath as he reached the pavement, savouring the sweetness and ridding his nostrils of Warne's dust and pretence. His generation would sign up willingly. *It's the old ones who'll sit and fight from the safety of their armchairs.*

AUGUST 1914, HAMPSHIRE

The leaves on the copper beeches danced in the breeze; the late summer sun lighting on them produced a warm glow. Nicholas had always loved them more than any other trees on his estate, even in their bare winter form. Now, leaving the cab at the gate and savouring the walk along his own drive, he saw them afresh. He used to meet Paul under these branches when they were hardly more than boys, taking a chess set or pack of cards to play seemingly endless games bathed by the warm August Hampshire sun. There'd be no time for such frivolity now.

He told Nanny that he was signing up almost as soon as he reached the house, before anyone else. She'd been so proud at the thought of him putting his name down. "You'll look a picture in your uniform. Have all those mesdemoiselles waving their handkerchiefs at you. Be careful you don't come back with one of them on your arm."

"I promise." Only recently had Nicholas been able to address his former governess and not feel seven—and—a—half again. Even though he towered over her, she would always seem the grown—up one of the pair. "I hope to be off training in just a few weeks, which will give me time enough to set my affairs here straight. There are plenty of safe pairs of hands to entrust things into."

"Young Mr. Haskell will keep a steady eye on things," Nanny said, fiddling with her knitting. No doubt those fingers would be employed producing socks or scarves or who knew what else over the next few months. "You'll be back come the spring, in time to see the lambs over at Longlea." She made the pronouncement as if it were a certainty, as sure as Christmas Day falling on December the twenty—fifth.

"I hope so." As Nicholas spoke the words, he felt a prophetic jolt, and knew it was all a lie. Somewhere inside—heart or brain, he couldn't be sure—he was certain they were in for a long campaign. Leaving the old lady with her wool and her thoughts, he went out into the gentle light to find Paul.

As he walked down the path back to the beech avenue an instantly recognisable, elegant figure came to meet him, a gun hanging off its shoulder and an uncharacteristically serious look on its handsome face.

"You'll sign up?" Paul didn't attempt any small talk; it wasn't their way. They usually met three times a week, if Nicholas was down in Hampshire, and those meetings always began with a litany of business, action taken or to be considered on the estate, successes and failures. Only when all the business was dealt with would Paul take a beer, relax for half an hour and indulge in chit—chat. A discussion of parish scandal, something which might have been called gossip if they'd been female, a brief harking back to the days when they'd traded all their secrets over that chess board. True to form, Paul hit straight at the crux of things now.

Nicholas wasn't sure if the question was an order—*you do this for the honour of the estate, I can't*—or some sort of expression of jealousy, that he could go where the other man could only dream of. He couldn't dare hope it was the beginnings of a plea for him not to go.

"It's my duty." The words seemed inadequate, barely expressing anything Nicholas felt. Yes, he was bound by duty, but there were other considerations. He was, he knew, running away from conflict as much as running towards it.

"I'll look after things." Paul's eyes registered something which might have been offence.

Nicholas replied hastily. "Of course you will. I've never doubted it." He'd doubted his own intentions, of course.

He cast a sidelong glance at Paul, wondering what expectations he'd have. The estate manager wore his business face, a cool, clear eye surveying the fields, maybe weighing up the chances of the next pheasant brood surviving the depredation of fox or buzzard. Sometimes Paul spoke of his family, an occasional glimpse into a world not bounded by rents or yields; would one of his brothers or cousins be taking the King's shilling? "Will Tom volunteer?"

"He's not told me one way or the other. They'll want medical men, of course, especially ones who know about bones." Paul smiled, as he always did on the rare occasions he mentioned his older brother. Nicholas had often wished *he'd* been blessed with a younger sibling to hold him in such high regard. "They'll want ones who know how to deal with heads. And what goes on inside them as well." Paul scuffed with his boots at a weed which had dared to poke its nose up in the immaculate gravel.

"Do you wish that you'd been able to get over there?" Nicholas immediately bit his tongue. Why on earth had he felt the need to ask such a stupid question? But the words were out and beyond recall, maybe as lethal to friendship as a vixen among the nestlings.

"Good God, no. If it wasn't for this," Paul tapped his gammy leg, "I'd have to find some other way to avoid it. I'd drive ambulances, or crack codes, run messages night and day if I had to. I *couldn't* go and fight." The sea—green eyes looked straight into Nicholas's deep grey ones, hiding nothing, baring Paul's very soul.

"Why?" Relieved that their friendship hadn't fallen at the first hurdle of his clumsy questioning, shocked at his friend's uncharacteristic candour, Nicholas rushed in again.

"I couldn't shoot another man, or bayonet him." Paul's face, normally ruddy from fresh air and exercise, had turned as pale as the hawthorn blossom they'd collected as boys. He ran his fingers through his fine, dark hair.

Nicholas tried to keep his eyes from admiring those long slender hands. Hands he'd seen wring the neck of a critically injured bird caught in the raspberry netting. Hands which could knock out, behead and gut a trout in thirty seconds. Hands which had tipped blossom into his, the gentle brush of fingers on palm remaining in Nicholas's mind long after the flowers had faded and lost their odour. "I see. I think I understand." He didn't, but he wouldn't judge out of ignorance or misapprehension. If Paul had his reasons, that was good enough.

11

"Do you? Then you see more than I do." A sad smile crossed Paul's face, like a cloud over the sun. They stood a while in silence, watching a kestrel quartering the field the other side of the beeches, both wary of words which could build a wall between them.

"I don't believe you're a coward, Paul. I've seen too much of your valour to make such a mistake." The village bully thrashed because of what he'd done to a harmless tramp who'd been holed up in the woods behind the church. The dog which had gone wild and worried the livestock—confronted and despatched, almost clinically.

Paul shrugged. "Maybe it takes a braver man to stay at home at times like this. Don't ask me to speculate on the nature of courage."

"How long have you felt this way?" Nicholas looked at the gun and the man who carried it. He'd thought they were close, that they knew each other as well as any pair of friends might, but now it seemed like he was talking to a stranger.

"All my life, or at least as far back as I can remember. Don't you recall when we were boys?"

"You never played at soldiers." It was true and the remembrance was blinding, a light on the Damascus road. Paul had always been the one to pretend that he tended the horses or the wounded. Maybe, at a pinch, he had driven the horse artillery and placed the guns. Never a foot soldier or an officer.

"I never did and I never will. I'm sorry if you despise me for it." Paul studied his boots. "You can find someone else to manage your estate when you return. I'll be

12

here—I daresay no one will want to steal me away, not if they know the real reason I'm not marching to the front."

"I don't want any other man to manage things here." Nicholas just managed to prevent himself stopping after 'any other man'. "Although what on earth do you do with the poachers?" Nicholas took the gun and put it to his shoulder, lining up on some imaginary target in the distance. "I hope to God they don't discover this is all for show and the man who carries it would never pull the trigger."

"I hope so, too. Luckily, the boy who helps keep the game has fewer scruples than I do. Still, if I meet one of our thieving friends at night, the glint of the barrel is usually enough to scare them off. Surprising how well bluster and a loud voice work." Paul took back the rifle, clearly seeing it only as a tool of his trade, not to be abused. Like a carpenter who could never take his precious hammer to another man's skull. "My mother always used to tell me to keep a face ready in a coffer by the door. One face for the world, and another for yourself."

Nicholas wouldn't let himself read into the remark all the things he desperately hoped to find there. On a day of revelations, what more about his friend was there still to be discussed? And what use was a veiled hint now, with his departure looming on the horizon? How could he bring himself to say *I know which face you wear for the poachers, Paul; which face do you wear for me?*

"That sounds like me when I visit my club, putting on a character with my overcoat." Nicholas cursed himself

13

for the small talk, but what choice did he have? Better to talk about anything rather than what he really wanted to say, now the eleventh hour was at hand. "I can be myself here at home, rather than the man who goes up to London pretending he cares about whatever his solicitor wants to show him."

"If you want me to deal direct with your solicitor while you're away, I'd give it my best shot. My father knew a bit about stocks and shares." The difficult subject had been skilfully avoided. They'd tacked onto another course now, although whether they were both purposefully avoiding the sharp rocks of Paul's inability to fight or something else lurking beneath the waters, it wasn't plain.

"I'll give you the power to act as you think fit." Nicholas avoided Paul's gaze, afraid to see either affection or indifference there. "I've always trusted you with this estate and I see no reason to alter that opinion now."

Paul's voice faltered. "I hope it's a short war. I fear it won't be, but I can hope."

Nicholas shrugged, afraid to speak now the word hope had been uttered. Why couldn't this conversation have happened months ago when there was, or at least there had appeared to be, time to explore where they really stood? Was he signing up just to prove to Paul he was more than just some feckless landowner who'd never had to put in a day's manual work in his life? That he too could be successful, heroic, all the things by which a man was accounted great? That there was some point and purpose to his life other than maintaining an estate for a son who would never appear?

You're trying to be Nanny's knight on a white charger, the poor country boy who turns out to be the hero of the tale. Nicholas ignored the voice of his conscience.

You want to be able to ride back here in glory and lay your medals and service history at his feet, like a slain dragon or the Apples of the Hesperides. You want him to be astonished, so you can say the words you've hidden so long: I love you, Paul. I have since we were lads together.

Nicholas shivered, even though the evening was still warm. "I hope it'll be quickly won, for all our sakes." *Why wait? There may never be a dragon to lay at his feet. You may never return. Tell him.* "Shall we meet tomorrow so we can get our plans clear? For the estate?" The coward's way out, keeping to business.

Paul nodded. "Aye, there's our own plan of campaign to set out—we'll have to work out how to maintain this place when every able—bodied lad in the county is off to volunteer. I'll come ready with some ideas."

Nicholas shook Paul's hand, dismissing him with a nod in lieu of the words he knew might betray him—if not in substance then in tone. He watched Paul walk briskly towards the copse where the path led down to the cottage he kept, memorising his gait, the colour of his hair, all the little things he could cling to out in France or Belgium. Tomorrow they would speak of business, and that would be all. Nothing else could even dare speak its name.

MARCH 1915, NEAR YPRES

He was still alive, unless he'd died and this was hell. No, it had to be real; Nicholas wouldn't be telling himself how damned lucky he was, otherwise. Luck? Given the average length of time an officer lasted out here it was more like a miracle, some guardian angel watching over him, sitting at his shoulder and fending off bullets and shells. It didn't do to keep thinking about why one man survived and the one next to him in the line went down, how inseparable friends were parted by a sniper's sharp aim. Fairness didn't come into it, nor logic, and no one could possibly understand who wasn't living in its midst.

This was no chivalric tournament. There was no white charger and the only dragon roared with the voice of field artillery.

The first letter from Paul had come within days of Nicholas reaching his training camp. Stiff, formal, and full of business, it had required an answer to one particular question about the state of the stable roof, one Nicholas was sure the man could have answered for himself. Paul still deferred to his absent employer; soon he'd be getting into the swing of making weightier decisions as a matter of course, the reporting back almost a formality.

Unless. Unless the question about the roof had been asked to ensure that Nicholas replied; almost every letter had seemed to contain something which needed a response. He'd tried not to raise his hopes about that, any more than he tried to raise his hopes that the British really were gaining ground against the Hun. Wondering if there was hidden significance in Paul's words was as pointless as hoping the war would be over by Christmas 1916, let alone this. And there was always what seemed like a last—minute, casual addendum. *What is it like there? Have you seen anything of Belgium? Do you see much of the horses?*

What is it like there? That same question came often, but how could Nicholas reply with any degree of truth? It wasn't even worth the attempt, as it would all get censored, anyway. *Water and lice, that's what it's like, Paul. Our two greatest preoccupations.*

He'd crafted the words in his heart often enough, the lines he never dared commit to paper. *Somehow, my heart's got hardened to the killing, the buzz of the flies and the awful smell of corrupted flesh; it's the water gets me down. It soaks your boots, makes your puttees like flannels. It falls down in curtains, fills the air with damp cold, bites to my bones.* Sometimes he'd been brave enough to commit a more candid word to a postscript, but mainly he dreamed of saying them face to face, over a pint of beer. *I never imagined I'd fantasise about a dry shirt and socks.*

Paul's letters were much more prosaic, although equally lacking in anything really weighty. He'd be keeping any real trouble close to his chest, dealing with it quietly and efficiently. The sensation of not wanting to shock and worry the other person cut both ways. *We've had terrible trouble with the drains* was often as troubling as things got in the weekly report. Still, Nicholas searched the letters for hidden meaning. *Did the ladies at church say*

17

they miss you greatly, something all the congregation would concur with mean *I miss you, and I wish I'd had the guts to tell you before you went?*

But even if Nicholas could find the words to convey both horror and affection past the censor's black pen, he wasn't sure he'd impose either on Paul—how could anyone comprehend the trenches or forbidden love who'd not experienced either of them? Boys in his unit would stand, dazed at first sight of the living conditions. They'd signed up to serve King George, for valour and a bit of glamour, perhaps, not to stand for hours up to their knees in water, or picking the vermin from their trouser seams. Nor to listen to the cries coming over from no man's land, where some poor soul was a long time dying.

Strange how these same lads now looked up to Lieutenant Southwell as an exemplar, how Sergeant Miller always used him as an illustration of what a soldier should aspire to. "You just follow what the Lieutenant does and you won't go too far wrong." Miller was a good bloke and, God willing, he'd see the thing out. He seemed to have the luck, unlike Lieutenant Jenkins.

The last few months Nicholas had shared his part of the dugout—a series of dugouts—with Jenkins. The officer had been sent home, half his face taken off by a shell, although the rest of him remained intact, including his mind. Whether that would prove to be a blessing or a curse God alone knew. Nicholas had been awaiting the replacement with trepidation, dreading some silly—ass, 'I'll win this thing single—handed' type of idiot. Maybe this would be the point where Nicholas's patience ran out and he'd end up strangling his fellow Lieutenant with his bare hands.

"The new officer's here, Lieutenant Southwell." Miller's tones sounded almost prophetic, breaking into Nicholas's thoughts while he was supposed to be keeping an eye on what was happening at the far end of the trench.

"Very good, Sergeant." Nicholas produced the most encouraging smile he could manage in the circumstances.

"He's stowing his kit at the moment, sir, then he'll be reporting to you."

"I'll meet him in our billet." Best to make sure this new chap was adequately prepared and couldn't dishearten the troops with an ill—timed word or glance. Nicholas took a deep breath before entering what passed for officers' quarters, expecting to find some wet— behind—the—ears pup.

He found, instead, a revelation. The replacement officer could have been Paul Haskell's cousin, so similar was the colouring and build, the easy grace of movement. He introduced himself as Phillip Taylor, slung down his things where Jenkins's used to be and sat down on the bed as if he had been ensconced in this part of this trench all his life.

"Pleased to have you with us. Been out here long?" Nicholas heard someone speaking and realised it must be himself, mechanically producing the sort of thing which needed to be said in the circumstances.

"Two months. I was further down the line. Not that it makes a lot of difference, which particular piece of hell you count as your own." The newcomer spoke cheerily, a grin lightening the words he spoke. He cast a glance around the little billet. "Not bad. Seen worse. Not as good as home but it'll do."

"Nowhere is. I never thought I'd yearn to see a good, solid oak tree…" Nicholas couldn't quite believe how the words were pouring from his mouth. He was well aware that the men called him taciturn, and now he was blethering on like a girl, revealing more about himself than he had in all the time he'd been with Jenkins.

"Or have a pair of good, dry socks." Phillip adjusted his puttees, producing an effect which might impress the men with its smartness and would equally make some attempt to keep out the wet and cold. An experienced hand, then.

"Dear God, I'm starting to be desperate for those." Desperate for something else too, dreams of Paul still burning into his brain but never manifesting as more than a quick bit of self—pleasure. No painted whores for him.

Phillip smiled again. "We'll go and buy some on leave. Saville Row tailors or some nice French equivalent."

"You should meet the men." Nicholas rose, confused at the emotions pounding in his brain and heart.

The next few hours seemed to pass in the usual way, the everyday routine at the forefront of his mind, while in the background an unsettling song played. Into a world depicted in the sepia tones of a photograph, a world bounded by shellfire and unearthly shrieks, had come cheery tones and the sudden remembrance of longed—

for delights. Nicholas had expected to be unsettled by the arrival of another officer, but not in this way.

Sometimes over the last six months he'd caught a glimpse of some well—built, handsome lad, sun—kissed from working in the fields, and had made himself concentrate hard on matters in hand, to force himself not to respond. That had been easy for a body used to being controlled, a face accustomed to hiding its true emotions and a conscience which needed to stay true to Paul. How was he going to cope now, with Phillip's face so close, his breath sounding in the darkness of their quarters, his presence more deadly than the snipers' bullets?

"They seem a steady bunch, the men." They'd returned to quarters and Phillip lay back on his bunk, seemingly as much at ease as if they were at Warne's with nothing more unsettling than a Boat Race dinner going on outside.

"They are. Though God alone knows why they should be here when..." Nicholas stopped himself short.

"When lesser men are propping up the bar, waxing lyrical about how they'd finish off the Hun within the month?" Phillip laughed, a soft bitter chuckle. "There was one old buffer, calling on my mother the day before I signed up, who nearly got the toe of my boot up his arse. Would have done if we hadn't been in mixed company."

"That bad?"

"I'd never heard such jingoistic rubbish."

The conversation about old bores and their view of the world flowed naturally. Two officers, thrown together by no more than a freak chance of posting, immediately

21

recognised in each other something special. Nicholas had found—for the first time since he'd been strolling along the beech walk with Paul—someone he wanted to talk to, someone he wanted to know about and to be known by, whatever the risk. Maybe it was because he could half—close his eyes and think it was Paul there with him, chatting happily as they'd chatted as boys. Maybe it was already the burgeoning of something different.

The conversation ran on, as they sought to put each other into some sort of context outside of mud and barbed wire. Nicholas spoke of his home, never referring to Paul as anything more than his estate manager. "And you? What did you do before this?"

Phillip ran his hands through his hair. "Attempted to make sure no one ever realised I was just playing at being a lawyer. I was—I am—at Lincoln's Inn. My father would like me to take silk one day."

"And is that what you want?"

"I think so. I used to think I'd like to cloister myself away in Oxford, living for nothing but the love of learning, but the world—and my father in particular—had other ideas."

Nicholas cradled his mug of tea, the brew turning tepid and almost undrinkable. He didn't care; he had something else to lift his spirits, now. "Oxford? Which college?"

"Brasenose. Don't tell me you were there? I'd have remembered you, I'm sure." Phillip smiled, draining his own brew, which must have been just as vile.

"Not Brasenose. Wadham. I read Greats." Nicholas dreaded being asked why he'd chosen the subject and what use he'd put it to. It was the sort of question his father had asked him too often.

"That's far too clever for me. I took English with the rest of the dimwits." Phillip laid down his cup with a sigh that seemed to come up from his boots. "Miss the old place, though."

"So do I." They sat in the not—quite silence, the never—to—be silence. Nicholas thought fondly of his table in Hall, the line of bright shining faces, full of hope. How many of those faces still smiled and how many had gone the way of all flesh along this very line? "Will you ever go back?"

"Maybe. When I'm old and grey and crusty, and father's gone. Then I'll have no expectations to live up to except my own. How about you? Never tempted by a garret in an ivy—encrusted ivory tower?"

"Too many memories in the old place for that—good and bad." Nicholas swallowed hard. Paul Haskell wasn't the only handsome face to have turned his head and one of them...one of them, combined with candlelight and too much wine had nearly been the cause of a night ending in disgrace. One day he might not be able to exercise the same degree of self—control. "If the right chance came up somewhere else, I might consider a university life, only not Oxford."

"I agree with you about the memories." A shadow passed over Phillip's face, some shade of troubles long gone. "So tell me all about your estate. Do you play the lord of the manor or has the twentieth century penetrated even the hedgerows?" Phillip smiled his dazzling smile and suddenly the darkness of Belgium lifted temporarily.

MAY 1915, NEAR YPRES

"You have to go home. You must be mad to want to stay here." Phillip smoothed his chin, easing fingers over the parts the razor had left raw.

"There's no one at home to go to. You know I've no close family." Nicholas stared at the letter from Colonel Johnstone, the one which virtually ordered him to get home and take a rest. There was little point in staying if Phillip had gone, anyway; better to go back to Hampshire and try to keep his hands to himself when he met Paul.

Phillip had been given leave, too and he seemed alight with some private, inner glow. "How about you? What have you planned?" Nicholas asked the question for formality's sake; the thought of Phillip enjoying a passionate reunion with some chit of a thing burned into his dreams, torturing his sleeping self.

"I'll be seeing family, of course, and..." Phillip considered his face in the mirror once more. Nicholas suddenly realised he was playing for time, weighing up his options. He'd seen that expression before—it spoke of utter candour. "And I have someone waiting for me, someone I'm very close to."

Nicholas had to fill the silence that clung to the coattails of that bald statement. "Not like you not to have mentioned her before." The strain in his voice seemed amplified by the tension which had descended between them.

"I didn't feel entirely sure I could, not up until now." Phillip finished his toilet and rolled down his sleeves. He turned, fixing the full piercing glare of his green eyes on his fellow officer. "You're a good man in a tight corner. Reliable. Can I rely on you now?"

"Of course." Nicholas awaited the revelation, the great secret he was to be entrusted with. Was Phillip laying siege to some other officer's wife, sapping her resolve and providing comfort while her man was miles away? If so, it was little wonder he wanted to get home.

"It's not a girl, at home. It's a man. Yes, I know I'm a bloody idiot telling you, but I trust you with my life, Nicholas. Have done every day since I got posted here. You're not going to shop me, are you?" Phillip ran his hands through his dark hair. "Not sure it wouldn't be worse if you told my parents than if you told the Colonel. He'd probably be more sympathetic so long as I'm not buggering Miller."

The unaccustomed coarseness made Nicholas wince, although he was sure its origin was nothing but Phillip's nerves masquerading as bravado. "I had no idea." Weak words, stupid sounding once they hit the air, yet it was all he could manage. If only he'd known, he might have said something. Sooner.

"I'm hardly likely to advertise it, am I? Fergal's a good sort—he's an engineer, working on ships' engines for Vospers. Wants to get to sea himself, the idiot." The deep affection apparent in Phillip's voice cut into Nicholas's heart. He'd never heard him speak this way, even about his family.

"Tell him to stay safe ashore." Nicholas forced himself to grin. "Enjoy your time together, God knows you deserve it. I won't tell anyone."

"Good man." Phillip thrust his hand forward to be shaken. "And you get yourself a bit of fun while you're at home, you old stick in the mud. Find a girl—not too nice or there'll be no fun at all to be had. Or a lad, if that's what you fancy." He cuffed Nicholas's arm. "At the very least, go out and get sloshed and forget all about this place for a while. Anyway, you can't fool me. You're secretly delighted to have the chance to go home, however much you hide it. And this chap Haskell who runs your place for you will be pleased to see you. Won't he be glad to bend your ear directly as opposed to long—distance?"

The flush running up Nicholas's neck caught him by surprise, the wild rush of blood to his ears making them hum worse than when the shells went over. He tried to respond but there seemed to be no communication between brain and voice. Please God he wouldn't have to end up telling the whole sorry tale.

"Oh God, Nicholas. I'm sorry." Phillip's hand briefly touched his fellow officer's face then fell away. "You don't need to say any more unless I've made a complete idiot of myself, in which case you can correct me with a few well—chosen words or a right to the jaw. I should have realised, from the way you mentioned him. At home I would have done—there are signs, aren't there? Does he know?"

Nicholas couldn't easily form a reply. Phillip was shining a searchlight into his soul, illuminating something that even *he* didn't realise ran so deep. Of course he wanted to see Paul again, no matter how much he also wanted to stay with Phillip. If he thought he had any realistic chance, he'd run straight back to Hampshire and drag him into the nearest bed. Even a haystack would do. He'd been dreaming of seducing Paul, long dark nights of fitful sleep under noisy night skies. Even these last few weeks, when he'd also been trying so hard not to think of getting his leg over Phillip. Far—off temptation had seemed a much more manageable threat than real and present danger.

"Does he know?"

"No."

"Then for God's sake find out if there's any chance he might feel the same and, if there is, tell him. I mean it. This leave." Phillip looked deadly serious, as if he was sending some young soldier out on a suicide mission. "There may not be a next time. Seize the chance."

"Maybe." Nicholas's hands shook; he steadied them on Phillip's arm. Why was everything such a bloody shambles?

JUNE 1915, HAMPSHIRE

Maybe. The word had re—echoed in Nicholas's mind all the way back from the continent and now, with Romsey station only minutes away, he still felt that uncertainty. He was certain Paul would be waiting in the road, having driven the trap up to collect him even though he had barely more than a pack to carry. He dreaded looking out of the window in case the carriage wasn't there. Or perhaps in case it was. Nicholas wasn't sure which would be worse.

All the way back to Blighty he'd found his thoughts confused. Paul. Phillip. One of them inclined to loving men but already spoken for. The other as free as a bird but an unknown quantity; available and yet, perhaps, unattainable. Both of them lodged in his heart.

"Mr. Southwell!" The tones were unmistakable, ringing in his ears before he'd got the carriage door open, a hand thrust into his for shaking no sooner than his feet had touched the platform. "It's good to have you home."

"Paul," Nicholas couldn't have used the name Haskell, not now that he had the man by the hand, and could bask in the glow of his welcoming smile. "You shouldn't have come. I could have walked."

"Nonsense. We couldn't have had you making the trek all the way to the house." Paul took his employer's baggage, swinging it along as if it were a child's school bag and loading it onto the carriage.

"The horses look well. You must be pleased with the replacement groom." They looked wonderful. Sleek, healthy and conspicuously avoiding anyone coming along and shipping them off abroad. Just as well; that would have broken Paul's heart. Nicholas thought of Belgium again and shivered.

"Put this blanket over your knees. You'll be cold with all this travelling." If Paul could read the real reason for Nicholas's discomfort, he was too much of a gentleman to mention it. "The lad's fine. Too young to sign up yet, so maybe this dreadful war will be finished while we're still getting the best from him."

"I'd be keeping my eye out for another lad to replace him, Paul. They'll be needing every lad they can get, soon." The conversation turned to the mundane affairs of estate, town or village—the sort of idle gossip he'd been looking forward to indulging in, although suddenly it felt stale and pointless. It was less like coming home than travelling away from it, but whether home was now the muddy plains or the close company of Phillip Taylor, Nicholas couldn't tell.

"Mr. Southwell, I asked if you'd want to inspect the accounts." Paul turned the trap in through the gates.

"I'm sorry, I was miles away. Yes, I'll take a brief look at them, but not this evening." Nicholas smiled, despite the heaviness pressing on his spirits. "And my name's Nicholas, or have you forgotten? I could do with a break from formality." He looked around at hawthorns snowed under with blossoms, a profusion of green leaves along the hedgerows. "Everything looks wonderful. You don't need me here at all."

Paul didn't reply at first, his attention carefully focussed on the driveway up to the house and round to the stables. As they at last came to a halt, he slipped down from his seat and said, "Don't say that," before handing the reins over to the stable lad.

The simple words cut into Nicholas like a bayonet. The entire journey from the station he'd vacillated between thinking of the man at his side and of the man who'd been his constant companion the last few weeks. Both of whom he desired and neither of whom he was sure would have him. The injunction *Tell him* still rang in his brain, but now he was here, he wasn't sure he could do it. *What a bloody coward you are.*

"Nicholas, are you feeling all right?" Paul's voice, tinged with deep concern and something which was more than that—Nicholas didn't dare think of what it might be—nudged him out of his thoughts.

"I'm fine," he snapped, "just tired from the journey." The sudden look of hurt in his friend's eyes brought him up short. "I'm sorry. I'm tired to the bones, Paul, more than I've ever been in my whole life."

"Then I'll not bother you with anything more than the essentials." Paul's hand was gentle on Nicholas's arm. "Rest all you want. I'll make sure you're not disturbed unnecessarily."

"Don't wrap me in wool, I'm not a child. I'll deal with the business as normal."

Paul removed his hand, as suddenly as if it had been slapped away. "As you wish, Mr. Southwell. Business as

31

normal. Summon me when you want to see the accounts." He turned on his heel, off into the stables.

You're such a fool. Nicholas stood watching Paul go, unable to call him back.

For the next few days, business wasn't as normal. Paul became aloof, emphasising his position as a mere estate manager and therefore subservient to the owner of the land. The easy conversations over a glass or two of beer, the recollections of which had warmed Nicholas during nights of unmitigated misery in Belgium, had ended. They were further apart now than when the breadth of the English Channel had separated them. Nicholas couldn't work out whether it was the war or his own treacherous heart which had spoiled things.

He soon thought about putting in a request to go back early, willing to return to one living hell rather than endure another of his own making. He'd begun to work out how what excuse he'd make when the telephone call came, Phillip's voice crackling down the line and bringing some much needed light into his darkness.

"There's no chance you've got a day or three to spare, is there? Fergal's gone up to Scapa Flow on some hush— hush project or other and I'm at a loose end. I'd hired a cottage on the Test where we were going, you know, to pretend we were doing some fly fishing. It's down your neck of the woods and I wondered if you'd like to come along." There was a pregnant pause. "Always assuming you haven't got more exciting things to do."

Nicholas swallowed hard before answering. "No, it's business as usual here. What about your family? Won't they think it odd you going away almost as soon as you've got there?"

"No. I've insisted I have to get some peace and quiet. You can hear the bloody guns out in the street on a quiet evening, Nicholas. Never thought I'd say I appreciated the artillery. Excellent excuse to get away."

Nicholas could almost hear the smile down the phone. "I'll get my fishing tackle packed. Where will I meet you?"

"Give me your address now and I'll pick you up en route. Got the old bus from father, and mother's loaded a ton of stuff. We'll feast like kings." Phillip's usual friendly, rambling style felt comforting after Paul's terse conversation of the last few days. "I can be down there after lunch."

The rest of the conversation was prosaic, detailed instructions on how to find Nicholas's house, if they should bring a gun for game as well as the fishing rods? His worries only crystallised as he got around to packing his small case. What would Paul say about his abrupt departure? And why the hell should that matter anymore, anyway?

***

"I'm pleased you could come. I'd have felt a bit lonely here on my own." Phillip stared over his glass, looking not at Nicholas for once, but at the white plastered walls of the cottage's living room. It had proved smaller than they'd expected, just the cosy side of cramped, but it suited them well enough. Now they sat on either side of

33

the little table in the parlour, bathed in the golden rays of the westering sun.

"There's a distinct difference between solitude and loneliness. The one doesn't necessarily mean the other." God knew Nicholas was aware of that; he'd been living it the last few days, surrounded by people he thought he loved and lonelier than he'd ever been.

This setting was idyllic, the cottage garden stretching down to the river banks, with the opportunity to be up early and tempting the trout. He used to fish a lot with Paul, especially when they were boys, although he couldn't even remember the last time they'd sat on the bank together, doing little else but concentrating on the little floats bobbing and dancing. He didn't anticipate them doing so again.

"You've never spoken a truer word." Phillip sipped his wine again, picking up the last morsel of cheese from his plate and savouring it. "You keep an excellent larder and your cook packs a superb picnic. That's the best meal I've had since I got home."

"Bread and cheese and pickle? Hardly the feast fit for a king you spoke of."

"It was for me. And this wine," Phillip turned the glass to catch the light from the candles, "is as fine as anything I had pre—war. Your good health."

"And yours."

When the last of the food was gone, they could rise from the table and leave the washing up for another time, a deliberate two fingers at the discipline they'd temporarily left behind. Nicholas settled himself in an old

34

but comfortable armchair. There were two neat bedrooms upstairs, each with a pair of single beds, suggesting this was a bachelor's haunt, for hunting and fishing and not for dallying with women. They'd naturally stowed their stuff in separate rooms even though they'd shared a billet for so long. Nicholas had found sleeping alone in his room at home unsettling; he'd been looking forward to not having someone living in the same space all the time, yet it hadn't turned out to be the pleasure he'd anticipated.

As he'd unpacked his bag in the little cottage bedroom, he'd looked at the single bed and known he would find it as hard to sleep these next few nights as it had been back on the estate. If he'd expected it to be so much easier to get a decent rest in Hampshire, with just the song of owls for a lullaby, he'd been mistaken. The relative silence was unsettling.

Not that there was anything even resembling silence when Phillip was around. "Last night, back in London, I dreamed I was dead." He'd turned the conversation off at sudden right angles. "Honest truth."

"Good God." That might answer one question. Nicholas had wondered, ever since Phillip's car had pulled up in his drive, exactly why the man had wanted him to come here. Any man who'd been dreaming of death might be reluctant to be alone. "If I'd dreamed that, the shock might well have actually killed me."

"It was a funny dream, really. Not frightening this time, not like..." Phillip broke off, perhaps reluctant to describe some of the horrors which had come to him in previous dreams.

"Don't feel you need to tell me about it, if it's too painful."

"No, I don't mind telling you." Phillip smiled, settling further into his chair. "I've always been prone to rather vivid night time visions. Before I knew you, before I was transferred, I'd dream Fergal had died and no one had let me know. I couldn't tell him, even if I'd dared."

If Nicholas reached out, he could touch Phillip's arm, but he wouldn't, on principle. Not while Fergal's name was still fresh on the man's lips, no matter how much the wine was trying to persuade him otherwise.

"I'll stop being mawkish and tell you about this dream." Phillip drained his glass and laid it on the floor. "I was an angel and I'd been given orders to report to the Archangel Raphael. He sounded just like Colonel Johnstone. Maybe it was the tone of absolute but merciful authority."

"I can imagine Nelson spoke in the same tones." Everybody admired Johnstone; Nicholas had been damned lucky to serve under him.

"You daft beggar." Phillip smiled, as happy as Nicholas had ever seen him. "Anyway, Raphael gave me a ticking off. Said that my expression might fool old ladies and maidens but it cut no ice with him. Apparently I was supposed to be your guardian angel and I was letting the side down." The imitation of the accent was uncanny; this could easily have been Johnstone talking about a rifleman with a spot of rust on his gun.

36

"I can't imagine you as *anyone's* guardian angel. Heaven must have been running short on recruits if they'd stooped that low." Nicholas eased out of his boots and stretched his legs out before the fire; dear God, it was wonderful to have dry, warm feet. He'd earned this. They'd both earned it. "According to Raphael, how were you supposed to have discharged your responsibility improperly?"

"I've no idea. I remember pleading that I'd nudged you out of the way of a bayonet at Givenchy. Made it go straight into a tree so it couldn't harm anyone."

"I never fought at Givenchy."

"I know that, but dreams hardly abound with a proper sense of logic, do they? Then Raphael started on about some bloody incident with an ice cream. I think I'd got you covered in it, all to put some poor girl off the scent. She was making a nuisance of herself and I felt it was my guardian—like duty to get her away." Phillip grinned, running his elegant fingers thorough his dark hair. "It made sense in my dream, even if it doesn't now."

"Quite right, too." Nicholas drained his glass, holding it out to be refilled. "Is there any wine left?"

"What did your last servant die of?" Phillip twisted in his chair, reaching for the carafe. "Enough for half a glass each and a finger or two for later."

"Thank you." Nicholas took a sip. "I'm grateful for whatever happened with the ice cream. Who'd want some pouting filly hanging around, who only fancied me for my name or money?"

"Ah, but you wouldn't object to some prancing stallion, would you?" Phillip swirled his drink, observing it closely as if it alone could answer the question. "What you want is a nice chap, with plenty of patience and kindness."

Nicholas stopped himself voicing his thoughts out loud. *I've got one of those at home and the only time I wanted to give him the slightest inkling of how I felt everything went arse over tip. I've got another one next to me, right now, and he's got the 'already sold' label on.*

"I'm assuming, by the fact you're here and didn't have a pressing need to stay at home, that you didn't actually tell him. Your chap, Haskell." Phillip's voice was solicitous, soothing.

"I tried to." It sounded pathetic. "It was like we couldn't really talk to each other anymore. Not even as friends. Now he's taken it on himself to simply be my estate manager, strictly business and nothing else." Nicholas stared at the fire, trying not to meet his friend's eye. "I envy you and your Fergal. Knowing where you are with someone must be wonderful. Did you see him at all when you were in London?"

Phillip stared into his glass again. "For an afternoon, in the company of all my family, including a younger sister who tried to monopolise him. We barely had a minute alone—I might as well have been back in Ypres."

"Don't say that." The wine had loosened Nicholas's tongue but he was beyond caring. At least he could talk to Phillip, frankly; there was no one else he could be so candid with. "I assume, at least, you were still on speaking terms, unlike Paul and me. Hostilities commenced and the barbed wire put up."

"Oh yes, but a fat lot of good that does. Having him close enough to talk to means having him close enough to touch and being unable to do so. I was thinking all the time about the big bed upstairs and how we couldn't get into it." Phillip slammed down his glass onto the chair arm. "Might never get into the bloody thing together again, not with him being away till I go back. Missed chances, never to be retaken."

Missed chances. Aye, the both of them. "If you really were my guardian angel, what chances would you grant me?" The wine was making Nicholas bolder as well as garrulous; bold enough to leave his seat and sprawl at Phillip's feet, in front of the hearth.

"The chance for you to be whole and well, and with this wretched war out of your system." Phillip's face was flushed—a carafe of white wine begun on empty stomachs had seemed an excellent idea earlier on. It might still be if it made the memories of mortars and mud recede even further. "It's what I'd wish for any of us." Phillip emptied the last of the wine into his friend's glass. "Happy days, old man. Or as happy as we can make them. Oh, and a happy belated birthday, too."

"Thank you." It had been Nicholas's thirtieth birthday two days after he'd got home, although all he'd had was a card from Nanny, more suitable to a boy than a man, a perfunctory note from Paul wishing him many happy returns, and a blue—iced cake from the kitchens. Only Phillip had bothered to make a fuss of the event.

"I have some things for you from mother," Phillip produced a small parcel, clearly labelled with Nicholas's name. "I was meant to take them back to Ypres with me but I thought it would be better you had them here."

Nicholas smiled, incredulous at the stunning generosity he was being shown by a family who only knew of him from their son's report. He knew the depths of Phillip's generosity, his surprising openness; maybe this was a trait the whole family shared. He picked at the wrappings with unsteady fingers. "Chocolates, she's sent me chocolates. Wrapped to within an inch of their lives so that they would survive the journey back." Tears began to well in Nicholas's eyes, maudlin tears germinated by the bleakness of his own household's celebration of the event and watered by the alcohol. "You must thank your mother for this. I'll write as soon as I can, but will you thank her, too? You've a way with words."

Phillip smiled tenderly and touched his friend's arm. "Aye, I will that. Only don't write from here. The family think I'm having a few days on my own. Don't shatter their illusions."

The obvious questions died on Nicholas's lips. *Why didn't you tell them? Does Fergal even know you've brought a friend?* Something had changed, subtly, just as it had done when Phillip had come to collect him; they'd crossed into some sort of new territory and he wasn't sure he could get his bearings yet.

"And now you should tell me what I can give you." Phillip's voice was mellow and gentle. "You promised you'd drop me a line and let me know, when we were on leave and where the war couldn't reach us. I note that you didn't, unless the letter got lost."

"I'm sorry, I should have, but everything's been so…" Nicholas didn't bother to finish the sentence. "My mind's been on other things."

"Well, your mind can get itself back to really important matters now. If Haskell wants to restrict himself to being the estate manager, then let him damn well manage in your absence, if he can."

"Oh, I'd never doubt his capabilities. He's had plenty of practice." Perhaps that was it; some sort of resentment in Paul at 'the squire's' return home to lord it over him once more? No, that was unfair. Paul had been more than solicitous. *Rest all you want. I'll make sure you're not disturbed unnecessarily.* The words rang in Nicholas's ears, reminding him whose off—handedness had caused the estrangement. Stupid, condemnatory words; he'd ignore them.

"So give me my answer now. What present would be fitting for my closest friend?"

Any words that Nicholas wanted to speak got caught in his throat at hearing 'closest friend'. Where and when had Fergal gone out of that equation? His alcohol—befuddled brain couldn't cope with such subtleties, not on top of trying to separate thoughts of Paul and Phillip, the two men becoming muddled in his mind. Hadn't he been Paul's best friend for twenty—odd years and hadn't that been shot to pieces? He should have asked the question when they stood under the copper beeches the

41

previous year. He could never dare broach the subject now.

Nicholas was aware of a voice speaking some strange words, a voice which sounded like his and seemed to come out of his own mouth, although where the question had come from, who knew? Maybe his brain didn't know who it was addressing any more. "Could I have a kiss? For friendship's sake, at least?"

Phillip gasped, clearly more amused than shocked. "It's not what I expected but it's not unreasonable." He leaned down, taking Nicholas's face in his hands, gently caressing the cheeks and soothing away the lines which had formed there these last few months under the constant shelling and hum of battle. "Of course you can have a kiss. One for your birthday and one for luck." He kissed Nicholas tenderly, once on the cheek then lips on lips, wine or affection or both making the brief embrace edge beyond the boundaries of friendship and into the territory of affection.

Nicholas, aware of his quickening heartbeat, leaned up to risk another brief kiss. "Not just for luck—it feels like an act of mercy, as well. Thank you."

"You daft beggar." Phillip returned another kiss, eyes alight with something like mischief and a strange emotion Nicholas couldn't put a name to as he'd not seen it so close up before. "What you really need is one for every year of your age. Like the bumps when we were at school. I think I owe you another twenty—seven kisses." Phillip only bestowed another two, though, before pulling back, still smiling.

"That's twenty—five you still have to repay. Maybe I should save the others up, and call them in when the world seems particularly dark."

"No," Phillip looked even more playful. "Cash them in now, if you want them. This bank only has a branch in England. Nothing available back in Belgium."

If this was just the wine talking, it sounded remarkably sober and sensible, crystallising Nicholas's thoughts. Maybe Fergal hadn't really gone to Scapa Flow. Maybe he'd found some better option, closer to home, some nice bloke who wasn't always so far out of reach. Something had clearly happened, some sea change undergone between his revelatory conversation with Phillip in Belgium and now.

Any resolution Nicholas had left was being gradually surrendered yard by yard, trench by trench. He brought Phillip's face closer again, kissing without counting whether they were getting any nearer to his birthday number. His mouth was open now, letting Phillip's invading tongue plunder all it wanted; this had gone beyond a joke, if it had ever been that simple. "You don't need to do any of this, not if you don't want to. You've gone above and beyond the call of comradely duty." One last attempt at decency towards Fergal, before it was too late. Or was it one last attempt at decency to Paul?

"You are such an idiot. Of course I want to. I took a shine to you when we first met—I can't remember the exact point where friendship ended and affection took over, although I suspect it was only when I realised you had the same sort of feelings. Perhaps it was the only bloody good thing that happened while we were out in Ypres." He tugged at Nicholas's shirt, bringing him closer again and making his intentions clearer in one simple movement. "Still thought I hadn't got a chance, what with this Haskell of yours."

"Paul Haskell's no rival to you anymore." If Nicholas expected some reference to Fergal not being a rival to him, it didn't seem like it was going to come. Phillip clearly played to his own agenda and Nicholas wasn't going to be privy to it yet.

"Then I've got an even better present for you. If you want it."

Nicholas needed no second invitation. Part of him had wanted Phillip from that first night they'd met; Paul had been miles away then, Phillip within sight, touch and smell. Now the same conditions applied and no threat of court martial or anything else was going to get in the way. And no matter how scared he felt at losing his virginity—the wine couldn't entirely take that fear away—Phillip surely had experience enough for them both.

Simple kisses and caresses turned into the first tentative explorations of clothes and then flesh, slowly pushing back the barbed wire of reticence and gaining the precious ground of confidence and trust. Phillip clearly knew what he was about and he didn't seem to be concerned that Nicholas was making it all up as he went along, trying to give the illusion of understanding and experience.

"Nicholas," Phillip's voice was deep and hoarser than usual, "how far does this go? Whatever you ask of me, you can have it."

Nicholas wasn't sure what he should or could ask for. *Whatever you do with Fergal* would risk some sort of a scene, the need for an explanation about why Fergal wasn't getting his due. "I'll have whatever you want to give me." That seemed the safest answer.

"I'm not sure we have world enough and time for that." Phillip stopped, looking carefully into Nicholas's eyes and evidently spotting the lack of confidence there. "Dear God, you've never had sex, have you? I assumed your Haskell was just another man. I didn't realise he was *the* man. The watershed."

Nicholas sighed, resting his head against Phillip's neck, drinking in the smell of sweat, cologne and masculinity. "I'm sorry. I should have said, but I feel such a bloody fool about it. Lieutenant Southwell, thirty years old and never dipped his nib."

"Not even with a girl?" Thank goodness there was no incredulity in Phillip's voice, just the need to establish the facts rather than judge them.

"Good God, no. Never." Nicholas felt a sudden pang at the thought of another complication. He'd assumed that other men who felt as he did would feel *exactly* as he did. He'd never considered there might be variations on the theme. "You?"

"Not exactly. I was very nearly engaged once to quite a flighty filly, so I think I got a bit more experience than plenty of young men just courting. Not quite the lot—that was strictly reserved for after the wedding breakfast. But then I met this chap…"

"Fergal?" Nicholas regretted saying the name as soon as he'd spoken.

"No—o. Fergal came along a bit later and found I was a *fait accompli*. Thanks to Laurence. He took me slowly along the path to enlightenment—Fergal would have dashed me down it at full pelt and probably sent me straight back into Millicent's arms, engagement ring at the ready." Phillip lightly stroked Nicholas's hair. "I'll be a safe guide. We won't rush."

Nicholas shivered, despite the warmth of the fire and the warmth of Phillip's arms. "I've lived so long rejecting the new in favour of the safe. You'd have thought this last year would have toughened me up but I'm frightened, Phillip. Part of me says we should seize this day and the other part says that none of this is real—that anything we do here and now with the threat of the war over us we'll live to regret when this bloody madness is over." He forced himself not to break down. It was only right to be canny; if Phillip was to wake in the morning with the wrong man in his bed, regretting he'd let the wine seduce him into betraying Fergal, then even their friendship would count for nothing.

"Sleep on it, then. If it feels as right sober as it does drunk, we'll seize the chance at once." Phillip took another kiss, then, yawning and stretching, let Nicholas out of his grip. "Dear God, I'm tired. I think I'm off to my bed. See you in the morning."

"I'll just stay up a while longer. I'll make sure the fire's banked down." Nicholas stared into the diminishing flames, confused. They'd come here as friends, they'd taken the first tentative steps along the road to being lovers, and now where had they got to? Clearly whether they had sex or not wasn't as momentous a thing to Phillip as it was to him; maybe the man's experience had made him blasé, forgetting how significant the first time might be. Or perhaps Phillip's sudden departure for bed had been to cover his own disappointment and to ensure he didn't force Nicholas's hand, a valiant act under twin fire from his own desires and whatever had gone wrong with Fergal.

Or maybe Phillip was simply promiscuous, and any available body could be taken or left. Nicholas wouldn't let himself believe that. His verdict seemed to be confirmed when he went upstairs and found Phillip had abandoned his own quarters and was already fast asleep on the other bed, just as if they were back in Ypres.

***

They finished the last of the birthday chocolates the next afternoon, strolling through fields and along avenues of cypresses piercing the blue sky like green steeples. They'd breakfasted in a constrained sort of semi—silence, reluctant to touch on the previous evening's conversation, but an hour or two down on the river, catching their lunch, had restored their spirits.

47

Nicholas had woken still unsure, unable to decide what he was really feeling. Love? He'd been certain he only had that for Paul and what he'd felt for Phillip was some mixture of misdirected lust and overenthusiastic friendship. Now he couldn't put a name to what he felt for either of the men.

The grey morning sky hadn't helped, either. It looked more like Verdun than the valley of the Test but, as they'd landed the second of an eventual half—dozen trout, the sun had come out, the clouds dissolving into tatters, and Phillip had looked up from where he knelt over their catch with a glorious smile. Nicholas had known then what his decision had to be.

The cottage looked less bachelor haunt than lover's bower, now Nicholas saw it through sentimental and anticipatory eyes. A glimpse of heaven with hell just across the Channel. They'd finished off the trout cold for dinner, with salad and a bottle of wine, before climbing the creaking stairs two at a time. They'd not even discussed whether Nicholas would seize his chance; the question and its answer were written in their faces.

Once in their shared room, Nicholas stretched out on his bed, enjoying the sight of Phillip standing by the wash bowl, casually stripping his shirt, dousing then towelling his chest. He'd seen that sight before, only this time he didn't have to hold his desires in check. Slipping into bed together drunk had been narrowly avoided—over the top and into no man's land was going to be done sober.

"Phillip," Nicholas reached for his friend's hand, "is your offer still available?"

"The one you've been secretly grinning about all afternoon?" Phillip squeezed the hand which held his, smiling and easing himself onto the bed. "It is, unconditionally. I think this would be the perfect occasion to discharge your weapon, especially as it'll be the first time. My all—out assault on your virginity can wait until you've recovered." He undid the topmost of Nicholas's shirt buttons, going down the line with care, stripping him as gently as a valet might. "We'll just take it one small step at a time." His mouth was on Nicholas's chest now, kissing and tasting the trembling flesh.

Nicholas, who'd braved bullet and bayonet, bomb and blast, paled at the thought of having to return to Belgium with Phillip at his side and face their men afterwards. "We've world enough and time for small steps, then?"

"Of course we have, don't be daft. Now get these things off." Phillip tugged at his friend's trousers. "If you get a move on, we'll have time for a nap before the light goes entirely. And then..." Phillip took another kiss.

"And then?"

"If you're happy, we can try the main course. You'll get a very small taster of it in about," Phillip mimed the act of thinking very hard about a calculation, just as Sergeant Miller did when he was considering a bombardment of artillery, "seven minutes, more if you've got the same amount of self—control you've shown as an officer. If that's all a façade, it could be about ninety seconds." Phillip was clearly aware of the exact state of play and seemed keen to bring things to a swift conclusion. They would have all the night to explore

49

further what making love could mean. "Then said main course can be delivered—on a repeating basis if you wish—any time between saying goodnight to morning light."

"You mean that?" If Nicholas had anticipated some hurried, fumbling affair, he'd underestimated both Phillip's stamina and his guile. He breathed hard and slow, trying not to spoil everything with a premature discharge of his weapon.

"Of course I do. And don't worry about going back to Belgium and the men seeing the raddled state you'll be in. They'll be envious that you've managed to get yourself holed up all leave with some classy tart. I won't let on about the truth." Phillip's grin was wicked, urgent, with a touch of desperation. "Now stop rambling and let me get on with things. Lie back and think of England if you must."

Nicholas lay back, thinking of everything but England, until all thoughts disappeared as the explosion rocked his whole world.

***

"Phillip." It must have been the best part of two hours later, although Nicholas couldn't be sure. Phillip lay dozing, dark hair flopped over his eyes. "Wake up."

"Hm? What?" Phillip shot bolt upright, like he was expecting the call to leave his bunk and get into the action. "Oh, hell." He lay down again, snuggling back into Nicholas's arms. "I must have been dreaming we were back there."

50

"We will be, soon enough. Don't rush it." Nicholas caressed his friend's hair.

"Now, are you trying to nudge the waiter into providing the next course?"

"Not at present. This diner is satiated, at least for now."

"Leave it for breakfast then…" Phillip rolled over, nestling down and clearly preparing for sleep. The question on Nicholas's tongue—the question he'd been mulling over the last hour—lay there, unspoken. Perhaps that was fit and right; this was no time to ask why Phillip had spent himself here, in this bed and not with Fergal. He'd delay the question if it meant more time making love together.

Hell, it had been stunning. Nothing could have prepared Nicholas for the sheer magnitude of the event—the faces of the men who'd swaggered from the local brothels when they'd had some leave behind the lines looked haggard and coarse compared to the beatific smile Phillip had worn when he'd come.

Nicholas watched Phillip's chest rise and fall, the curve of his neck and the colour of his skin. Had he fallen in love with him like he'd assumed he'd fallen for Paul? Was this just another layer of complication to add to the mess he'd got himself into? Phillip had called his name at the height of ecstasy, head thrown back and eyes tight shut— "Nicholas!" spoken with pride and possession.

"Phillip?" Nicholas no more than breathed the words into his lover's ear, afraid to wake him.

But Phillip wasn't asleep—he turned, smiling. "Don't even ask. Of course we can." He pulled Nicholas towards him, smothering his face with languid and then passionate kisses before the man had the chance to say, "How did you know what I wanted?"

"I can read you like a book. It'll be fine, I promise you." Phillip's voice, deep and low in his ear, increased Nicholas's excitement. "You can take me whenever you want. I'll be ready."

***

There was a lot less to pack onto Phillip's car now; the food had almost all been consumed, the wine was just a pleasant memory and the only additional baggage was some fish. And the load of memories, of course. Three days of companionship, walking and fishing; two nights of romance and sex; never a mention of Fergal, nor one of Paul after the first evening. Nagging guilt was left behind, not wanted on the journey—Nicholas had lost the weight of remorse the second time they'd made love. He wasn't promised to Paul, and Fergal had become a nebulous, unmentioned, faraway presence, so why should he regret the happiness he and Phillip had found?

"Ready?" Phillip had the engine running, and was just making sure everything was stowed away neatly.

"Fit to go, if that's what you mean. Never prepared to leave here if I had the choice." Nicholas drew Phillip towards him for one—maybe last—kiss.

"But we don't have any choice in the matter, do we?" Phillip ruffled his lover's hair. "Maybe next time." He took one last look at the cottage. "Come on. If we don't go now, we might be tempted to stay forever."

Nicholas climbed into the passenger seat, determined not to look back. "Shame we can't. Stay, I mean."

Phillip got in to his seat, slipping on his driving gloves and looking thoughtful. "We've got duties elsewhere, haven't we? Belgium, your estate, my Fergal." He eased the car along the dirt track towards the road, evidently not aware of the knife he'd just driven into Nicholas's heart.

SEPTEMBER 1915, ARTOIS

Nicholas left the torrid, waterlogged rabbit burrow which served as their quarters, to walk along the line of his men. He made a daily round to see for himself their position, the mess the latest bombardment had made of their trench. He smiled, made the odd joke, produced a light for a Woodbine, and left a feeling of renewed hope and vigour among those he'd addressed. Strange how much he'd grown up this last year; much more so than he'd done in the previous twenty—odd.

You'll be a fine young man one day, Master Nicholas. His nanny's voice still rang in his ears, although when they'd spoken during his leave her grasp on reality seemed to have become tenuous.

You went out there a boy but you've come back a man. Losing a grip on reality she might have been, but she'd been spot on with those words. On days like this, he thought of Nanny's picturesque view of the martial world, the one she'd drummed into him as a boy and the one she'd clung to all her life. She still imagined knights in armour galloping between the lines, as naturally at home on the bleak mud of Belgium as they had been at Agincourt.

For Nanny, and for many like her, the brutality of barbed wire, machine guns and horses blinded by gas, had been translated into a fairy tale romance of white lance and white charger. Nicholas hadn't disabused her of the notion and he wasn't sure he'd ever have the heart to do so. Even the pallid description of trench life he'd tried to give Paul the last night he'd been home—of being in a state of perpetual alert combined with mind—numbing boredom—wasn't one he wanted to share much further.

Paul.

There'd been a slight thaw in their relations, between returning from the cottage and setting off for Belgium again. Maybe it was because Nicholas felt less strained, less desperate, the delights of his satiated nights with Phillip still coursing in his veins. Maybe Paul had had the opportunity to mellow. Whatever the cause, they'd parted on almost friendly terms and their correspondence had taken up almost where it left off, as if the visit home had never happened.

Nicholas watched the post arrive, wondering if one of Paul's letters would be there. The men were abuzz with excitement at the thought of a note from a sweetheart, one to be pored over time and again, every word savoured as if it were holy writ.

"Anything for me?" Nicholas stopped young Dixon in his tracks.

"Sorry, sir." Dixon held up his pack, as if he expected his commanding officer to demand it be lain out for kit inspection.

Nicholas noticed there was one for Phillip, in his mother's distinctive, flowery hand. He smiled, knowing that it would be full of gossip, stories which would be shared with him as well, even though he'd no real knowledge of the characters involved. Letters from Fergal had never been shared, no matter how hard Nicholas' eyes had burned into them from the other bunk, desperate to know what he spoke about and how he phrased it. Maybe they'd originated some code before they'd even come here, *My mother sends her love* meaning *I miss you more than ever*. He wondered if they'd been pragmatic enough to work out a code for *I was lonely. There was this officer and I couldn't help getting into his bed. I'm sorry*. Now he always made sure Phillip read his letters in private.

Things had changed after Hampshire, as they should have known they would from the moment Phillip had dropped Nicholas home, the pair suddenly unable to look one another in the eye as they shook hands and said their farewells. They'd not spoken about those days, not once in the months since, as if by never referring to them would mean they'd never happened. But the consequences had remained. There'd never be the same freedom between the two of them again, no matter how politely they'd said goodbye or how business—like they'd been resuming their working relationship in the front line. Nicholas blamed it all on the war, of course, the constant pressure having made him lose his moral compass. Dear God, how could any man keep a sense of what was decent when they'd had to live like this?

As soon as Nicholas came through the pinned up blanket which passed for a door, he knew something was amiss. Phillip, ashen, stood in the middle of the floor with a piece of paper in his hand, the look of happiness which usually accompanied the arrival of the post noticeable by its absence. Nicholas spoke softly but resisted laying a hand on his friend's arm. "What's up?

Phillip passed his mother's letter over, clearly unable to find any adequate words to explain why he was doing it. Nicholas began to read, despite the fact that this was obviously intensely personal—the piece of paper actually exchanging hands was ominous.

I am so very sorry to have to break the news like this. If only I could be with you and speak these words, but I have to commit them to paper, my dearest boy. I hope that you can read between the lines and find my deepest love for you there. We had news today from your friend Fergal's ship; he had us listed as next of kin because of all the problems with his mother. I don't know if he ever told you that, but I think in the end it was wise. I will have to contact her next, although I think it might be better if I visit. Poor soul.

Last time they'd heard, Fergal had just got his wish to go to sea, guarding the fishing fleet from U—Boat attack. God knew how long this news had taken to travel back to England and out again.

By all this, you will be able to guess what I have to say. He is dead, killed by a shell. It was apparently swift and merciful, for which we must be grateful. They are sending his things back here and I will keep some of them for you, as a memento of your friendship.

I have no adequate words to describe how sad I am and how much I wish to be with you to console you. I pray to God as I write this that Nicholas will be able to give you the comfort you need at this time. He seems like such a good friend and I hope he proves so.

He could read no more. Phillip had slumped onto the bunk; Nicholas took his place alongside him, clumsily putting an arm about the man, the most intimate contact they'd had since the local church bells had struck four in the morning that last night in the cottage by the river. Phillip buried his face in his friend's tunic, his tears drenching the material more effectively than the French rain. Nicholas could fool himself into thinking he was anointing it with the oil of friendship and making a declaration of the once—sacred nature of their amity. Just once, he kissed the dark hair that rested beneath his chin and held Phillip as tightly as he dared.

"I feel as if it's all my fault, somehow." Phillip shuddered, great waves of grief heaving through him. "If I hadn't been so blasé back in that little cottage, this mightn't have happened. Almost as if I laughed in the face of fate and it's turned and had its revenge on me."

"Then it's my fault as well." Nicholas kept his voice low. "You didn't lead me astray. I gave myself willingly and knowingly." Knowing exactly what he was doing, and as a result the shade of Fergal had hung over the pair of them ever since, a dark cloud to dampen even the fondest memories. Now there was a tiny flicker of hope, shining in some dim recess of his brain. Once Phillip got over his grief, once he could lay down the burden of guilt, once this stupid war came to an end, then maybe they could find some way forward together. Life could be as it had been those idyllic few days by the river.

"No! No, I don't blame you at all. You weren't to know what had happened beforehand and I didn't see fit to

58

enlighten you at the time. You must have thought we'd parted." Phillip's tears had soon stopped, his stiff upper lip reapplied. "We'd argued, not long before I rang you. Bloody stupid, really—my sister was gabbling away at our family gathering, the one where I got so annoyed at not having Fergal to myself. Apparently she'd seen him out and about with some girl and wanted to know if it was his fiancée. I took it into my head to confront him about it and we ended up in a blazing row. He went off in a huff, saying I obviously didn't trust him so there was no point in continuing and I came running to you. Seems he couldn't trust *me*. See? All my bloody fault."

Nicholas swallowed hard, keeping down the swell of despair, ignoring the awful thought that perhaps he'd just been used at the cottage, a means of getting revenge on Fergal, or of keeping Phillip satiated while he got his mind clear about the man he really loved. "Did you manage to clear the air before you came back off leave?" It was the best Nicholas could do—any other question would be too painful.

Phillip nodded. "A letter was waiting for me when I returned to London. Fergal said he'd been a fool for being so touchy. The girl was his cousin, over from Dublin, and he'd been looking after her. He'd have explained everything at the time if I hadn't gone off the deep end. By the time we met again, two days later, I'd heard the same story from another source, so I realised what a complete bastard I'd been."

Nicholas couldn't be certain how much of what he was being told was true, but he wasn't going to fight over it at this point. His grip had loosened now; Phillip was slipping away, both figuratively and literally. "There was a rapprochement between you."

"There was. Tinged with guilt on both our parts, although mine was the more bitter." Phillip had eased out of Nicholas's grip entirely, now. "My behaviour was nothing to be proud of, was it? Tupping away like a prize ram at the slightest excuse. I'm sorry I implicated you in the whole sordid business."

Nicholas bit his tongue. *It wasn't a sordid business. They were the best few days of my life.*

"You've been so decent about it and I've been such a bastard." Words were pouring out of Phillip now. He sat with his elbows on his knees, head in hands, looking young and vulnerable. It took all Nicholas's composure not to embrace him again, although now the constraint wasn't just their location. Maybe Phillip was no longer worthy of complete trust. Nicholas would have depended on him, right to the end, out on the battlefield—but matters of the heart were a different matter. "I've not just felt guilty about Fergal; I've been worried about you these last few months. I abused your trust back in Hampshire—well, I've got my comeuppance right and proper, haven't I?"

"What happened between us in our bed was as much of my volition as yours. If I'd been so concerned about…" Nicholas whispered urgently, stopping himself using Fergal's name. That would have been too cruel. "About proprieties, I could have refused. But I didn't—when I screwed you, I was well aware of the implications."

60

Phillip looked up at his friend's unaccustomed use of barrack—room words. "Dear God, it sounds so brutal put like that. Thank you for being so sympathetic." His green eyes were cold now—bright emeralds, hard and lifeless.

"Isn't that what you wanted? For me to agree that what we did *was* wrong, was callous and brutal, if you care to put it like that?"

"I think I wanted sympathy." Phillip's voice was small, apprehensive.

"Sympathy? I think you want to wallow in blaming yourself because it somehow makes your betrayal of both of us feel better. I don't for a moment suppose that Fergal getting killed was God's punishment on you. The universe doesn't revolve around the doings of Phillip Taylor."

Nicholas regretted speaking as soon as the words were out and beyond recall. Phillip had never been angry with him before, not even in the heat of battle, but now he looked almost murderous with rage. "Thank you for reminding me of the fact. I find it *such* a comfort." Phillip rose, straightening his uniform. "I have to find Miller—he wants to discuss the new ammunition that's come through." He walked away, pausing only to pick up his hat and not once looking behind him.

"Phillip, I'm…" Nicholas's words were cut short as his friend spun on his heels.

"If you're going to apologise, don't waste your breath. I suspect everything you said is right. I just wish you'd chosen a better time to say it." Phillip fixed his cap in place. "Maybe there are no better times left."

Nicholas vaulted off the bunk, reaching out as Phillip edged back. "For God's sake, don't go and do anything stupid."

"Like put my head above the parapet?" Phillip screwed his face up into a rueful smile. "I wouldn't give my conscience the satisfaction. That would be the easy way out—much harder to live with what's in here." He tapped his forehead and left.

Nicholas listened as the voice, "Miller? Where's Sergeant Miller?" moved along the trench. Well, that was that. Any idea that there might be a way forward with Phillip at some point in the future would have to be put aside for now. Perhaps forever.

"Excuse me, Lieutenant Southwell."

Nicholas looked up to see Dixon standing in what passed for a door frame, a letter in his hand. "What is it?" he snapped, immediately regretting his harshness when the young soldier blanched. "Sorry, shouldn't have been short with you. Can I help?"

Dixon held out the letter. "There was one for you, sir. It had got muddled up with the next platoon's post. They've just sent it over." He saluted and made a hasty retreat.

Nicholas could guess who it was from without looking at the handwriting. Fate seemed to be determined to deal them all a heavy blow today. This would be Paul writing; one of his letters was due. He turned the envelope over in his hands for minutes before summoning up the courage to open it. Even then, he didn't dare look at the contents for what seemed an age. The feeling of impending disaster—or something equally devastating—was too strong.

Dear Nicholas, the letter began as normal, detailing the latest doings of the estate. Nicholas tried hard to concentrate on each line as it came, not to let his eyes run ahead in search of what he'd convinced himself was lurking in the text.

He'd reached the last paragraph, with nothing worse to read than a report of the entire locality being struck with chicken pox, and was ready to kick himself for his own stupid apprehension. He'd almost skimmed over the last part, sure that it would contain Paul's usual politely phrased best wishes; a single word brought him up short. Apologies. He read the paragraph again, now with his full attention. *It's taken him long enough to get around to this, but that lad on the estate, the one with the dodgy leg and the phobia about using guns, wants to apologise for his curtness when you were on leave. He gave me some cock—and—bull story about what had happened, but I suspect he's got an unnatural crush on you and had got himself worked up into a state about you being home. I'll keep an eye on him to make sure he doesn't step out of line again, but if you want him dismissed, I'd understand.*

There was only one person Nicholas knew of who could match Paul's description: the writer himself.

Nicholas steadied himself on the bunk. Why this confession now? Why not last September or this May, times when it would have made a difference, when all the squalid mess of the last few months could have been avoided?

63

Don't think like that. Nicholas shook himself, as if to shake out all the unhelpful feelings. Why should he be ungrateful if it had taken Paul so long to summon up the courage to speak—hadn't he been too cowardly even to broach the subject?

It's because of the news from the front. Nicholas felt the most likely answer dawn over him. The war hadn't been over by Christmas, the Hun hadn't been sent back to Germany with a bloody nose, and decent lads were dying in their thousands. Paul must have known that the chances of Nicholas getting home in one piece decreased every day; perhaps he could no longer keep silent.

He would need to start to draft a return letter. Soon, while the emotions still were dancing in his brain, before they were dulled by mud and misery. He'd started composing, was halfway through the first prosaic paragraph about estate business, and was preparing for the crucial middle section—*of course I wouldn't want him dismissed, I need to talk to him face to face, let me handle this when I get home*—when he caught sight of Mrs Taylor's letter, lying discarded on Phillip's bunk.

How could he be so fickle? He'd loved Paul when he thought he could never have him. He supposed he'd never stopped loving him, even when he'd lived and breathed Phillip. Even when he'd shared Phillip's bed, shared his body, shared his joy and shared his grief. Ten minutes ago he'd been germinating plans to win back Phillip's affections and now he was courting his rival again. Had he become some sort of soldier of romantic fortune, an amatory mercenary who'd take love wherever and whenever he found it?

"Bad news for you, too?"

Nicholas started. He'd not heard Phillip re—enter their quarters. He looked up, then down at Paul's letter, still tightly gripped in his hand. "No...yes...I don't know." Almost against his will, he held out the paper. "Skip over the first part; it's the end which matters." He still wasn't sure why he was doing this.

"Good God." Phillip looked in complete control of his emotions now. "I assume you don't actually have a lad on your estate who fancies you?"

"Aye." Nicholas dropped his voice. "It's a code for my eyes alone to understand."

"Then I appreciate you sharing it with me." The voice was clipped, controlled but not with the bitter edge Nicholas might have expected—Phillip's innate decency had resurfaced. "God's got a pretty odd sense of timing, hasn't he?" He smiled. "I'm sorry I snapped your head off earlier."

"You had every right to. I was pig—headed and callous."

"You were just what I needed. A kick up the backside. All the mourning in the world won't bring Fergal back." Phillip returned the letter to Nicholas's trembling hand. His face was set and fiercely brave, making it clear that any more discussion about his loss would be unwelcome. "I'm pleased for you, truly. If you manage to stay alive through this bloody farrago, then go back and make a proper life with him. Take the chance not all of us will get."

"And you?"

"What about me? If I survive, then I'll survive, if you get my drift." Phillip adjusted his cap. "Come on, you can compose your love letter this evening. Sergeant Miller doesn't like the look of half the stuff they've sent us and neither do I. There's work to do." He turned on his heels, leaving Nicholas to grab his cap, straighten his uniform and try to lick his thoughts into some semblance of order.

DECEMBER 1915, BEHIND THE LINES

"More wine?" Nicholas tilted the carafe towards Phillip's glass.

"Seems a shame to waste it." The little pension where they sat had a certain shabby charm; were it not for the sound of the guns in the distance, one could imagine oneself taking a little winter tour of Northern France prior to a proper Christmas at home. No such luck on that front—they'd been moved back here for re—training and amalgamating some "fresh from England and wet behind the ears" recruits into their company ranks, but they'd be back in the line by Christmas Eve at the latest. Still, the dispensation of one night's leave and somewhere clean and dry to spend it felt like a blessing.

"I've not tasted wine this good since..." Nicholas stopped just in time. "Since we were in that cottage" would have risked opening old wounds which seemed to have healed successfully weeks ago. "Since I can't remember when." He smiled. Life was good, if only for a brief while. His initial reply to Paul had brought another cleverly written response, "the lad on the estate" being grateful for his employer's understanding and Paul himself willing to act as broker in ensuring things were sorted out to everyone's satisfaction the next time he was home on leave. More code. More seeds of hope.

Matters with Phillip had settled down, too, the initial slightly uneasy truce maturing into renewed friendship, as it had been back in the spring.

"Monsieur, I have more of the same." The hostess came and hovered eagerly at their table. "I'd rather you had it than those filthy swine."

"So would I. Bring it along, please." Phillip's French was excellent, investing few words with a wealth of meaning. "It'll fortify us against ensuring *they* never get here."

A single stray flake of snow floated past the window; Nicholas shivered. "Here's to another Christmas it won't be over by."

"Maybe next year?" Phillip didn't sound convinced. "Still, we survived." He raised his glass, the last remains from the first carafe glinting in the candle's glow. "To absent friends."

"Absent friends." Nicholas chinked his glass against Phillip's; they drank in silence, the words "To Fergal" never spoken but somehow loud and clear between them. The fresh carafe arrived, glasses were topped up and a fresh round of toasts begun. By the time the last drop had been wrung into their glasses, a gentle glow wrapped them and the front seemed as distant as either London or Hampshire.

They refused brandies on the ground that the pair of them would never make it up the stairs if they succumbed. As it was, rising from the table was challenge enough, their blood seemingly having been replaced by pure alcohol; just reaching the stairs took all their self—control. By the time they'd entered their room and fallen onto their beds, they could hardly breathe from laughter and the effort of getting all the way up without collapsing.

"I didn't realise what a disgrace I'd become. I'd have not batted an eyelid at a bottle of wine, in my prime." Phillip kicked off his boots, flung himself down and lay, slightly swaying, on his bed. "Horribly out of practice."

Nicholas didn't quite trust himself to speak. He sat on his bed, not ready to lie down, either, in case it brought on another bout of dizziness. Phillip had turned to look at him, some strange, distantly familiar glint in his hazy green eyes. Nicholas might have taken some time to remember what that look meant, but when he did, the realisation was swift. And sobering.

Nicholas steeled himself. "I feel all in." He fussed with his bootlaces. "Once my head hits this pillow, I'll be away."

"If it was a shame to waste the wine, then it's equally a shame to waste these two beds." Phillip rolled to the edge of his bed, reaching out to touch Nicholas's knee. "Two old soldiers taking a bit of comfort together. Who's to condemn it?"

Apart from my already battered conscience? Apart from Paul? If Nicholas narrowed his eyes and let the wine do the seeing, it might almost be Paul on that other bed, head outlined by a single candle's glow, dark against light. Except this face could never be Paul's. The eyes were too knowing, with no sign of virgin ground yet to be explored—just an invitation to tread a path they'd gone down before. And enjoyed. Paul was far off and still just theoretical, no matter what the letters said; Phillip was here and real.

Phillip's hand was on Nicholas's face now, caressing the hollow lines of his cheeks. "You looked no more than a lad when we first met. I had no idea you were almost thirty." He leaned forward to steal a quick kiss; Nicholas shut his eyes and leaned into the embrace which came with it. "You look a man now." Phillip kissed him again.

Nicholas's conscience made one last attempt to waylay him, but wine, loneliness and the consciousness that he owed Phillip something blew away any doubts. They could both be dead in a week's time. They were both alive now and the bed was soft, so soft.

"Come on then." Nicholas pulled Phillip back with him, rolling together onto the counterpane. If the wine had affected their moral judgment, it hadn't dulled their physical responses—hard and eager, grinding and rough, but with a surprising tenderness that the trenches hadn't dulled. After long days and nights of abstinence, they quickly slaked themselves in a torrent of passion.

"You have no idea of how much I want you." Phillip's forehead pressed against his friend's as hot sweet kisses rained down onto Nicholas's face.

"Then have me." Nicholas spoke the words in tones of surrender, but he wasn't yielding against his will. Who was going to blame him except himself? And he'd lived with his own moral code for long enough now to make himself and it forbearing, if wary, bedfellows.

Afterwards, exhausted by passion spent and finding a peace they could find nowhere else, they slept. Nicholas's last thoughts before he succumbed to slumber were the memories of Phillip lying back on the bed, laughing and urging him to try discharging his weapon once more, as he'd already discharged it to both their satisfactions. Recollections of how ecstatic—quietly, constrainedly ecstatic, befitting the thin walls and narrow beds—Phillip had been when he'd come. How beautiful he'd appeared, on the verge of sleep, like an angel with a raddle mark on him. And how they'd both pretended not to notice when, at the height of bliss, Phillip had whispered, "Fergal."

JANUARY 1916, ARTOIS

Advance. Retreat. The war progressed like some enormous chess game doomed to end in stalemate. Fourteen months Nicholas had been out here, and now he was only a few miles from where he'd started and not in the 'right' direction. They were getting ready for another big push, although he had to pretend to his men that he felt this one would actually be worthwhile. How many men's lives were one hundred yards of land worth?

He and Phillip were back to being on as good terms as they'd ever been, his fellow officer regarding their night in the little pension as simply an outward symbol of their reconciliation. He gave no indication of demanding more, of wanting to renew a romantic relationship if they ever both made it home. Though they never spoke of it, Phillip gave the impression that he knew Paul should always take precedence, just as his Fergal had always been first.

Paul's letters still came with their neatly cryptic messages, and neatly cryptic replies went back, but each word—received or sent—gnawed at Nicholas's heart. How could he be so perfidious? Where was the noble knight on the white charger he'd dreamed of being? There was another letter, too, to prey on his mind. One from Phillip, which had been pressed into his hand almost casually, with an airy, "Read this if by any chance I don't make it back one day." Nicholas kept it tucked inside his vest, petrified not just that one day he'd be left to digest the contents alone, but that someone else might find it.

"Ready?" Nicholas's question had become routine, before anything of note, be it big push, relocation or just dealing with some unpleasantness among the men. Phillip's answer was always the same. "Aye, as ready as I'll ever be." Private words shared in their quarters or spoken at the junction of a trench; the routine of question and answer almost a talisman against harm.

"Ready?" Nicholas repeated the question, cutting through Phillip's unusual preoccupation with cleaning his pistol.

"Eh? Aye. Ready." If Phillip had noticed the deviation from hallowed custom he didn't show it. Nicholas had taken note—the cold vice—like grip on his stomach and the awful, stupidly superstitious thought, "He broke the charm, the good luck's run away," unsettling him worse than the distant rumble of artillery.

"Come on. Let's be at them." Nicholas couldn't bear to think any more on it—no man could afford to go over the top without all his wits about him.

"I'm ready as I'll ever be." Phillip's voice was cheery, but the magic words had come a fraction too late to be certain to appease fate.

FEBRUARY 1916

"Sir, sir!" Sergeant Miller came flying through the trench oblivious to the cursing he occasioned from the men he bumped into or trod on. He barged into the officers' quarters and nearly sent Nicholas arse over tip.

"What is it, Miller? And where are your manners, if not your discipline?" Phillip's voice—rarely raised—was harsh.

"Gone to fucking hell, sir." Miller gave a great grin, for once totally incorrect in all that he said or did, but no one was going to report him today. "It's all over, sir. They say it'll be done in a day or two. We'll be going home." Tears began to well in the grizzled officer's eye. "I'll see my little Mary again." He saluted and left.

Phillip couldn't stop giggling. "Why don't you kiss me, Nicholas, here within whistling distance of the men? Let's risk it just the once—we have to celebrate the day, and perhaps this would be the best way to do it."

Nicholas ignored his screaming conscience and let himself be kissed, knowing full well Phillip would try to seduce him again and he wouldn't fight back...

Nicholas woke up screaming. The pain in his right leg was all—consuming, the lights too bright, the room at first unfamiliar.

"Hush, there now. You've been dreaming again." A neat, starched and aproned nurse attended him.

Oh God, yes. He remembered now—at least in part. The war wasn't finished and it showed no sign of being finished at any time in the near future. They'd gone over the top and Miller had barely made it twenty yards before he'd gone down, hit in the head by shrapnel. Nicholas had hardly gone two strides further on when he'd been hit himself, victim of the same deadly bombardment; he should have known that the shells would get him one day. Funny how his first thought hadn't been the pain in his leg, although it must have hurt like stink, but, "At least now some other poor sod's going to have to write to Mrs. Miller." All the rest was a blur, a stream of events washing over him. Someone had got him back to the lines—had that been Paul? Paul's face had floated about on the edge of events, certainly.

No, not Paul's face, Phillip's. Strange how he could hardly tell them apart at times, unless he concentrated. It would have had to be Phillip; Paul was miles away...

"Nurse?" He struggled to sit up. "Is there any news of Lieutenant Taylor? From my company?"

"Oh, Lieutenant Southwell." The nurse's face wore a fond, exasperated look. "We've had this talk so often. He didn't make it back."

Of course. How could he have forgotten again? Maybe he'd taken a blow to the head as well as his leg and the doctors were hiding the fact he was losing his marbles. Or maybe he just didn't want to remember, to think of Phillip cold and in the ground. Nicholas hadn't seen him get hit but Colonel Johnstone had told him all about it, or as much as he'd felt right to tell.

Phillip's platoon had gone out first; chances were he'd been killed even before Nicholas's head had made its initial foray over the parapet. Such waste and devastation that day.

So it couldn't have been Phillip there, hovering over him; it must have been a hallucination. A wave of nausea struck Nicholas as his thoughts crystallised. Phillip dead and all the doubts and dilemmas gone with him. Only one decision now remained—how much to tell Paul of what had happened? For tell he would; he owed the man that. And confession might just pay off the debt to his own beleaguered conscience.

You're a bloody fool. Phillip's voice sounded in Nicholas's head. Why was he hearing words that Phillip had never spoken in life? Of course, the letter; Phillip's letter. Thank God they hadn't opened it when they brought him here. He'd found it still sealed, in his little bedside locker, shoved away by someone mercifully lacking in curiosity.

You're a bloody fool if you think you should tell Paul anything. What good would it do? Phillip was as forthright on the page as in life. Always the one to seize the moment and then sort out the mess afterwards, even from beyond the grave. *If you must make some big confession, do it twenty years down the line, if you're still on speaking terms. Maybe you'll both be able to laugh about it then. He's hardly going to expect you to be a blushing virgin, is he? Maybe you'd be no use to him if you were.* If Nicholas had expected to find his friend had left him an epistle full of sentiment, of regrets about what had happened either in England or France, he'd overestimated Phillip's gallantry.

76

Go home and tell him you love him, like I told you to do before. Don't make a hash of it this time, because you won't get a third chance. Things like that don't happen, not outside of those fairy tales your nanny told you. You're not a prince, your white charger's only a staff car and your suit of armour is bound about with puttees and webbing. The boy I knew is all grown up now. You're a soldier; you're a man.

Nicholas wondered whether Fergal had been left a similar letter, full of exhortations just to get on with life. He realised, with sudden regret, that he'd left nothing equivalent back home for Paul. Just formal papers, instructions and the like—a sizable chunk of money in his will, but nothing personal. Thank God there seemed a fair chance he'd be able to get back to Hampshire and say the words himself.

I nearly loved you, you know. That was the best I could do, given the extraordinary circumstances. I certainly held you in higher affection than anyone except Fergal. Maybe if I hadn't met him first then things would have been different, but I don't think I'd ever have really taken Paul's place in your heart, would I? Did you know you called his name when we made love (the second time) in that little cottage, when we were supposed to be having a few days fishing? I knew then I'd always be second fiddle.

Nicholas had learned every word of Phillip's letter by heart, could have recited it like the Paternoster or his daily orders. It had been the first thing he'd read when he'd come round and was the last thing he looked at every night. He supposed he should just bite the bullet and surrender to Phillip's advice, as he'd surrendered before—he'd always let the man take the lead, for good or ill. Which would it prove this time?

He'd already got his marching orders home, his leg too much of an impediment for life at the front. At least for the present he'd be more use at home, training the recruits, and before that, there'd be a few weeks of rest back in Hampshire; maybe at last he could get the mess cleared up.

MARCH 1916, HAMPHSIRE

Nicholas shifted in his seat. The train journey felt unusually bumpy today and ever since they'd passed through Winchester his leg had given him gyp. He was on the slow train now, thoughts turned in, not out. Paul would be waiting for him with the trap, just as he'd done last time. *I daren't make such a hash of things again.*

His eye caught a dazzling splash over in the water, where the clear and bubbling Test ambled down to the sea. Suddenly he was back in the cottage, remembering that deep comfy bed and Phillip's story of his strange dream. If the man really was somebody's guardian angel now, then perhaps he could spare a moment to keep a rein on Nicholas's tongue and bring things to a satisfactory conclusion.

Nicholas was up, fumbling with case and stick even before the train had rounded the bend into the station; he couldn't let Paul see him struggle to keep upright. He wedged himself against the carriage door, better to keep his balance. The trim figure on the platform, his eyes turned to scan the up track, could only be Paul, bouncing on his heels in anticipation, seemingly willing the train to go faster.

"Mr. Southwell!" Just like before, the voice bold and welcoming, Paul himself hared along the platform to wrest the door open. "It's good to have you home." He grabbed Nicholas's case, putting it down out of the man's way, then tentatively offering him an arm to help negotiate the treacherous gap to the platform.

Nicholas toyed with refusing any help—he wasn't an invalid, for God's sake—but his conscience brought him up sharp, as did the pain in his leg as he took the first step. "Thank you." He let himself be helped down, allowing Paul to rest his hand on the crook of his arm just a few seconds more than absolutely necessary. "Paul. Thank you for coming."

"I was worried that you'd insist on walking into town and trying to find transport there." Paul tipped his head towards Nicholas's stick. "I'm glad that's as bad as it got. Nasty, though."

"It's what they call a Blighty wound." Nicholas tapped his leg with his walking stick. "Sorry it took me a while to write about it."

"Don't apologise to me." Paul ran his hands through his hair. "All the staff were having kittens because I hadn't reported your usual weekly missive being safe in my hands. I knew the Germans would never finish you. You're too jammy for that."

"The devil's luck, maybe." They made steady progress out to the road, where the trap waited. "This is the same horse as last time. Has nobody twigged? Do you hide him when it's draft time?"

"Not quite. But he's mysteriously lame any time someone official comes snooping. Bit of a cough, too. Please don't enquire further." Paul absent-mindedly scratched behind the horse's ear. "Remember his partner? He wasn't as lucky—gone with the draft now. I don't suppose we'll see him back."

"No. And don't ask me what it's like for them out there." Nicholas patted the horse's strong neck. "It would break your heart." More words that echoed their last meeting, that disastrous—or was it wonderful?—leave.

"I bet it would. The groom's still with us, though. Too badly asthmatic, or so the doctors reckoned when he tried to sign up. He can beat me by a good ten yards over the fifty, but he's not fit enough to serve King George." Paul hefted the case onto the back of the trap. "Thank God for small mercies."

He turned, nodding towards Nicholas's leg. "And thank God for that, too. Is it callous to say I'm pleased? Better to have you off at some camp, training those poor sods, than out with them." He stopped, suddenly uncertain, another dangerous corner reached. "If I've spoken out of turn, forgive me. Perhaps you'd rather be out there fighting than here with..."

"No. No, I've seen enough to last a lifetime." Nicholas took off his hat, smoothing back his hair; he'd found the first grey one that morning. "This is where I need to be."

Paul nodded, as if that settled all that needed to be said for the moment. He motioned towards the passenger seat then offered a hand up. "Would it be easier if I got up top first and pulled?"

Sudden incongruous memories of Phillip, the cottage, a carafe of wine consumed, flooded back. He'd said something almost identical—different circumstances, naked on the bed. Nicholas couldn't help but laugh.

"What's so funny? Have I by accident hit upon the punch line of some filthy joke the men tell?" Paul leaped

81

up onto his seat then got down again. "I'll give you a hand. Bad leg up and then over. What is the matter?"

"I can't tell you, not now. In twenty years' time, I'll explain it all, I swear." Nicholas let himself be heaved up—not without difficulty, and a lot of pain, but he didn't want to let that show—then settled himself, pulling the rug over his knees. The unexpected puns, the laughter, Paul's querulous expression, swept Nicholas over the top and onto the new battlefield. "I valued your letters, every one."

Paul turned the horse's head towards the main road and the way home. "As I did your replies. I hope I didn't speak out of turn." He cast a quick glance at Nicholas, then turned his eyes back to the road.

"Out of turn? I've never been so pleased to read something." Nicholas wished they were home now—that they could have kept to business matters until they were somewhere safe and no longer had to speak in coded, guarded words. Somewhere they didn't have to use words at all, where all that Nicholas had learned with Phillip could be put into eloquent action. "I had no idea."

"Didn't you really?" Paul negotiated a path around a group of people wending their way home from market and turned the horse into a quieter road. "I suppose I was never brave enough to tell you. Face to face." Paul risked another glance at his friend, then a tentative smile.

If Nicholas had forgotten the blinding power of that smile, he remembered it now; relaxing his guard made his tongue looser than it should have been. "After what happened the last time we took this ride, I thought any chance I had was gone." He bit his tongue, inwardly cursing. Had he done it again, made the same fatal mistake? "I'm sorry, I was determined not to foul things up again. Looks like I've done just that."

"No, it's not your fault. I was too touchy. I remember snapping your head off—it was rude of me." Paul kept his eyes fixed on the road. "I should be the one to apologise."

"For what?"

"For thinking you looked down on me because I couldn't do what you'd done."

Nicholas wasn't sure he understood what was going on. "I realise I'm being terribly obtuse, Paul, but could you explain exactly what you mean?"

"Easy, boy." Paul slowly brought the horse to a halt, under an avenue of trees where the road widened. "I'd got it into my head that you didn't want to be home. All that 'You don't need me here' stuff and then haring off on holiday as soon as you'd arrived." He fiddled with the reins. "I was childish, like Christmas had come and the present I'd been dreaming about had been denied me. I was so looking forward to your return."

"Dear God. You must have thought I was such a bastard." Snapping, turning tail and running off to Phillip as soon as the opportunity came, instead of saying something and clearing the air. All his bravery kept for the front and nothing left to bring home. "I've never thought that. Never thought less of you for not trying to sign up, even if you'd been able to."

"I know that now. I even knew that then, but it was too late."

"I'm sorry?" Nicholas's head felt like it was about to explode.

"I knew that there was a chance you felt like I did, about...about us. And I guessed that you'd been too scared to say anything." Paul slapped the reins again, getting the horse moving. "I had a letter."

"A letter?" As Nicholas spoke the words, he knew that the next logical question would be pointless. The answer was obvious, although it had to be asked. "From whom?"

"Lieutenant Taylor. I saw that he was killed in action. I'm sorry about that, too. He seemed a good man."

Nicholas took a long look at his friend, but there didn't seem to be any hint of irony or sarcasm in what he said. "When did it arrive?"

"The day after you got back from your fishing trip. It said that you were an idiot." Paul took his eyes off the road, grinning at Nicholas. "He obviously knew you well."

"I'm glad I was held in such high regard."

"Oh, you were. For everything—your leadership, your bravery, everything except your ability to say what really mattered, when it mattered." Paul slowed the horse to nothing more than a brisk trot. The road began to wind here and both horse and driver had to have all their wits about them. "I suppose you talked a lot about home?"

"I got a bit maudlin and most of it came out." It was as close to the truth as Nicholas wanted to come at present. He shifted his leg, trying to find some ease. "I remember saying how I couldn't look down on you for your convictions, as I knew you weren't a coward." At least that was no word of a lie—he remembered the conversation clearly, he and Phillip resting in each other's arms, bodies shared and now sharing a cigarette and their deepest thoughts.

"Maudlin? Does that mean drunk? *In vino veritas* and all that?"

"Something along those lines." Drunk on making love for the first—and the second—time, certainly. *It wasn't making love, Nicholas. It was sex. Love's what I had with Fergal. That's what you could have with Paul.* Voice of conscience or voice of Phillip Taylor, it was talking loudly and talking sensibly.

"He also said you were the bravest man he'd ever met. He must have only seen you on the battlefield." Paul took a quick sidelong glance. "Unless you showed a distinctly manly streak wrestling with rod, fly and trout. You were never brave enough to say what you felt. Not to my face."

"I was afraid you'd take the butt end of your rifle to me. I couldn't know, Paul, could I? What man in his right mind would risk a rebuff and being up in front of the magistrate?" If it had been that simple, surely they'd have broached the subject long ago?

"Do you honestly think I'd have done that to you, even if I was mad enough not to welcome any advances?" Paul brought the horse to a halt again, easing the trap onto a little grass verge. "Couldn't you trust me?"

"I've trusted you all my life, or as long of it as I can remember. I'm not sure I ever trusted myself." Nicholas studied his hands. "All my life I've been scared of saying what I really felt, of being who I was deep inside."

"Wearing your own face when you went out of the door."

Nicholas started at the words—echoes of a painful conversation long ago—and at the hand lying on his arm. He looked up and into Paul's sea green eyes. "I had this mad idea of being some sort of knight in armour, laying my prowess in Belgium as an offering at your feet."

Paul tipped his head back and laughed. "Did you really think I needed that to be impressed? I'm no swooning maiden. It was only ever you I wanted, and I'm as much of a coward not to have told you. You have no idea how good it is to have you back here in one piece." He looked Nicholas in the eye, a look of such intensity it threatened to unman him.

"And here I am." Four words to express everything years of longing had accumulated. What use were further words now? They had, please God, plenty of time to share every corner of their hearts, if they wanted.

"Here you are." The simple phrase was spoken with great solemnity, almost as significant as wedding vows. "And here may you remain." Paul flicked the reins and urged the horse on again. They barely spoke the rest of the short journey to Nicholas's estate, just sharing a word or two about a tree which had come down in the wind or a gate on a neighbour's property which had at last been mended.

So they negotiated the difficult corners, geographical and metaphorical, and at last the house could just be seen, chimneys proud above the bare trees. It felt right this time, though; all the mixed emotions of the previous homecoming had disappeared. He really was home this time. As they turned into the gate, Nicholas motioned for Paul to stop the trap.

"Let me just take it in. It all feels too good to be true and I'm afraid I'll wake and find myself back in that damned hospital." He took a deep breath.

They sat still, unspeaking, for what seemed an age.

"Ready?" Paul spoke softly.

"Yes. Now I am." Nicholas smiled and received another glorious smile in return.

"Got your courage back? Ready to face the staff and have them fuss over that leg?" Paul nudged the horse forward, covering the ground slowly so that Nicholas could continue to take it all in.

"Courage? If you want to see courage, you wait until I've got you in my bed. *Then* you'll see gallantry above and beyond the call of duty." Nicholas stopped, cursing himself for having spoken aloud the thoughts he'd been nursing these last few minutes. If he'd expected a shocked reaction, he'd once again underestimated his friend, for Paul roared with laughter.

"Well, you've learned *something* out in Belgium, then. How soon can we decently engineer a practical demonstration?" He nudged the horse into a trot, as if the invitation to dalliance had made all other considerations disappear.

"Tonight. I'll have to let myself be wined and dined up to the hilt first, to make the staff feel as if I've come home properly. You'll be my guest, of course?"

Paul grinned. "I've already taken the liberty of asking Mrs. Rawlins to set an extra place at dinner. I said you wouldn't be wanting to eat alone and you couldn't yet face the prospect of entertaining. Everyone in the parish wants to come round and gawp at the hero, of course. And the leg."

"I bet they do." Mrs. Rawlins was going to have her work cut out. "It's not a wooden one, though. They won't feel they've got their money's worth."

Paul reached over and gently touched Nicholas's bad knee. "By God, it's good to hear you joking again. Now I know it's you home for real and not whoever came home last time in your stead."

You've hit the nail on the head, Paul. Whoever came home in June wasn't the boy who'd left the previous autumn. He got lost out in Belgium, on a wild goose chase. Or maybe he was waiting to outgrow the fairy tales before he could show his face again.

"Penny for your thoughts?" Paul swung the trap around the back of the house and slowed it to an elegant halt at the stables, where a young lad—awfully young— came out to attend the horse.

Nicholas waited until they'd climbed down, Paul solicitous but not overbearing, and the lad had led the horse away before replying. "I couldn't tell you them here. They're too obscene and one of the staff might come out at any moment. Later." He cuffed Paul's shoulder, withdrawing his hand none too soon, as Lewis the butler came to take his case and give the permanent staff's official welcome. Paul lingered, chipping in the odd word, clearly reluctant to be away, savouring every moment and hoarding them against delights to come. Only when another, even younger, lad had taken the baggage could they be alone again, standing on the step and looking down towards the copper beech walk.

"Nicholas, all this talk and none of it about business. You've distracted me from my duty. I haven't even asked if you'd want to inspect the accounts." Paul turned towards his friend, grinning broadly.

"To hell with the accounts, they'll keep." Nicholas smiled. "We've more important business to attend to."

"It's a shame I don't keep the books in my bedroom, although it could be arranged." Paul held out his hand to be shaken. "Go and rest. You look all in. I'll see you for dinner."

"I hope there's enough hot water for a good bath." Nicholas stretched, suddenly intensely weary. A hot bath would do his leg the power of good, too. "Don't feel you need to dress for dinner. I'll stick to the comfiest old jacket I can find."

"I'll make sure I wear something suitable for the occasion." Paul lowered his voice. "Although...what's the point if it's all going to come off? And what *will* you say to Lewis? I've not stayed over at the big house since I was a lad."

"I'll ask him to have a room made up for you as we'll be hitting the cellar and I wouldn't want you wandering home in the dark three sheets to the wind." The subterfuge added to the excitement. "You can be there for when he brings in the morning tea."

"Planning kicking me out of your bed before I've even got there?" Paul cuffed his friend's arm, then set off down the drive, whistling happily. Nicholas stayed for a while, watching him go, re—familiarising himself with the scene.

Home.

The raid on the cellar was fruitful and quite annoying to Lewis, as he'd wanted to choose the wine for the meal. They roused out three bottles; one to drink, one to send to the servants' hall and one (corked and ruined anyway) to pour out and pretend to have consumed. Nicholas hadn't even minded that his contribution to the raid was sitting on a chair and suggesting where Paul should look. Dinner was excellent, taken against a background of fire and candlelight, with nothing to be heard but the hooting of owls in the oaks and a distant fox screaming somewhere.

Conversation was mellow, as they caught up on events both sides of the Channel. Please God, there'd be plenty more evenings like this, sharing the parts of each other's lives spent separately, building up the jigsaw to complete the picture. Phillip's role in events remained understated; trusted colleague, valiant officer, skilful catcher of trout, writer of an unexpected letter. No more for now.

By the time Lewis had left them to enjoy a final port and a cigar, they were replete, contented and yet burning slowly with excitement. Sidelong glances and tentative smiles began to replace laughs and bonhomie. The bravado of the afternoon, the bold words spoken when travelling in the trap, had turned into shyness, boorish swagger replaced with tender flirtation.

"Shall we?" Nicholas leaned forward in his chair, inclining his head towards the door and, by implication, the staircase.

"It seems the right time."

They dimmed the light and banked down the fire, leaving Lewis the formality of restoring the room to a suitable condition for the night—they couldn't take all the man's pleasures away. The mounting sense of excitement even took Nicholas's mind off what a bloody awkward and laborious procedure climbing his own staircase was. They shared an overloud and slightly theatrical goodnight at the top, checking that no one was in sight. Then Paul quietly stole into Nicholas's room, laughing like a schoolboy.

"I feel like a nine—year—old setting off for a midnight feast. One that Nanny's expressly forbidden." Nicholas eased the door shut, whispering until any gap was firmly sealed. "Should I lock it?"

"Hm. Unlikely for Lewis to go wandering in the night, but it might be as well. You could always say you couldn't sleep with it open or something. Blame the war." Paul sat on the bed and slipped off his boots.

Nicholas forced himself not to look; he'd forgotten that Paul always needed boots to support his gammy leg. He remembered the slightly withered appearance it had, or at least had possessed when they were boys. He wasn't sure he'd seen it since then. Well, at least that would make the battered exterior of his own leg less of an issue. A pair of old crocks together.

"Penny for your thoughts this time?" Paul arranged his boots neatly under the bed.

"I'm not sure you'll like them. I was thinking we're a pair of old cripples." Nicholas eased into a chair and undid his brogues.

"We're meant for each other, then." Paul came over—slightly halt now that he was barefoot—and drew his friend up out of the chair. "I think I've been waiting for this for all my life. Ever since I can remember." He took Nicholas's face between his hands, pulled him closer and kissed him. A simple, almost chaste kiss, but Nicholas could still taste it even when the contact broke. Not the first kiss, the ground breaker and trailblazer, but maybe something more significant. The first kiss with the one who really mattered.

"I've been waiting for it, too. Won't take so long before the second one." Nicholas returned the kiss with passion, tongue probing and darting. No tentative slow testing of the waters and resting in the shallows, just a headlong plunge into the deep. And no need to worry that he was pressing on too swiftly—Paul's eager response made it clear he was happy with the pace.

"Not here. Over on the bed." Paul edged them backwards, never letting his grip on Nicholas loosen, nor the rain of kisses stop. His nimble, eager fingers were making short work of Nicholas's buttons, of tucked—in shirts and tucked—out jackets. And progress across the floor was easier with Paul supporting him. "A long time since I've seen you naked. You were a skinny streak of a thing then."

"We must have been boys." The sudden comprehension came over Nicholas that it would have been absolutely wrong to indulge these feelings back in the first stages of manhood. They'd have reared and kicked, hating the strange feelings, maybe resenting each other, feeling guilty at walking that dangerous and illegal path together. Better now, as men, entering any partnership with eyes open, aware of all the risks, and yet with the determination to cherish it. Aware of the sacredness both of life and of love.

Nicholas let himself be stripped, only fleetingly concerned about what Paul would think of his leg; the man would be far too sensible to make a fuss about it. Paul was being quick, efficient and incredibly erotic, like an amorous valet determined to arouse his master. Except no valet would surely ever attempt to disrobe the man he served while he was lying on a soft, warm eiderdown and the valet was kneeling over him, kissing and caressing every inch of flesh as it was revealed.

"My turn to have the pleasure. Or maybe it's yours." Nicholas was pleased they'd had the sense to load another log on the fire, so his goose bumps were only a result of excitement. There was nothing now but the fire's heat and Paul's lithe body to warm him. He eased his friend's clothes away, savouring the sight and touch of the skin, hot and soft against his fingers and lips.

What had Phillip once said? "There are plenty of men who choose to ride their colt or filly damn near fully

93

dressed, but where's the pleasure in that?" Nicholas concurred; he wanted to feel skin on skin, muscle on muscle, never forgetting that he had a man in his bed. Paul was almost naked now, just his shirt on and that completely undone.

"Do you know what you have to do?" Paul's voice was hoarse, trembling with excitement.

Nicholas felt tongue—tied. What if he said the wrong bloody thing now, when the fulfilment of his dreams seemed so close? Surely Paul couldn't still expect him to be some fumbling virgin who needed to be coaxed along? He played for time. "Do you?"

"That would entirely depend what we're about. None of your fancy continental nonsense. If we keep it at lying back and thinking of England, I'll be fine." Paul lay back, as good as his word, opening his legs as if to invite immediate consummation.

"Is that what you usually do?" Usually? How many men had Paul lain back for?

Phillip's imagined voice quickly rooted up the first shoots of jealousy. *You didn't wait for him; you can't expect him to have waited for you.* Still, he mustn't imply Paul was promiscuous and risk insulting the man. To be so close to the final assault, the concluding thrust which would win the ultimate victory...Nicholas couldn't risk defeat now by choosing the wrong word.

"Well, I'm not going to pretend that I've done enough of this to have a 'usual'. And I've not done it for a long time. Things might have changed since I was a lad." Paul grinned, for all the world like an overgrown and lascivious cherub.

"Can they have changed that much? Human anatomy remains the same." Nicholas stroked his friend's anatomy, shoulder to thigh, paying particular attention to the bits which would see most action.

"Accepted practice, then. Perhaps that's different, even if this," Paul ran his fingers across Nicholas's groin, "isn't. I promise to do more than just lie back and think, though. Can't leave you to do all the hard work."

"And you want to be the one doing the lying back?" How stupid, to be bandying words at such a time when they were both so excited, but Nicholas was still scared that he'd make a mistake, as he'd done so often, and spoil it all by imposing something uncomfortable on his lover.

Comfortable? Paul being comfortable! Hell, what was he to use? Phillip had always seemed to be prepared, with some salve or ointment he produced at the appropriate moment. Nicholas hadn't even thought about that contingency.

"Being on the receiving end suits me." Paul pulled his friend towards him, pressing their bodies together, kissing Nicholas's face with increasing urgency. "I want you. I want you now, stop making me wait."

"You can have me, once I work out how to...how to oil the gun carriage." Nicholas felt himself blushing.

"Is that all that's holding things up? I thought you were getting cold feet." Paul slipped out of their embrace. "Let me just get my trousers." He rummaged in the pockets, producing a little jar of something. Vaseline?

Nicholas couldn't quite tell in the dim light. Paul had come prepared; he should have had more faith in the man's ability to handle any situation. "This is the sort of thing that's needed for the job, unless my memory fails me."

"No, your memory's spot on." The flush was spreading from Nicholas's face to his neck at the thought of the next little awkward moment. There'd been no problem in stripping, in lying naked before his lover, but now, to be preparing himself so brazenly...it smacked of shamelessness, of whoring.

"If you're too shy I'll do it for you." Paul smiled a kindly, almost bashful smile. No teasing, no mockery there, just a sense of wonder at the shared adventure to come.

"You do that and we risk abject failure. I've some self—control but I'm not made of stone."

"I can see that." Paul took the object of his admiration in hand. "In fact, if there's a finer specimen of flesh and blood, I've yet to see it. If I'd known, I'd have spoken sooner." He stopped, suddenly serious, looking Nicolas straight in the eye. "I should have spoken sooner anyway, shouldn't I? I must have been blind not to recognise the signs. "

"Don't blame yourself. When you spoke about one face for the world and one for yourself, this is what you meant, wasn't it?" Nicholas reached for his friend's hand. "If we keep looking back at what might have been if we'd said this or what might have happened if we'd done that, then we'll drive ourselves mad."

"And put this fine state of affairs to waste, as well." Paul took Nicholas in hand again, stroking gently then letting him fall. "Come on." He leaned in for a kiss, a long lingering kiss, accompanied by gentle caresses and a small tattoo drummed on Nicholas's thigh.

In the end, Nicholas didn't know quite how he'd got himself ready. Those gentle kisses and tender touches had set them ablaze, the fiery flames consuming them and obliterating the need for any more talking. The excitement which, drowned in words, had dimmed, flared anew; they were hard, so hard and so determinedly excited. One of them had used the jar of Vaseline and primed Nicholas ready; he'd been too drunk with desire— desire at last to be fulfilled—to remember who or how. Maybe it had been both of them, a rush of fingers and palms.

And now, prepared, he took Paul. Not too long and loud protestations of everlasting love—not yet, maybe not ever—but to an accompaniment of sighs and whispers. *At last. I've waited so long. Glad you're home and where you should be.*

Afterwards they lay, too keyed up to sleep, talking softly. The night was proving mild and the fire threw out enough heat still to be comfortable, the lambent glow highlighting the honey tones of Paul's flesh. And their shared passion had produced warmth that the coldest of nights would have been hard pressed to cool.

"Happy?" Paul, curled in the crook of Nicholas's arm drew lazy circles on his friend's stomach. "To be home? To be here?"

97

"Of course. Both. At times I thought I'd never be happy again." Nicholas inched his hand down towards his wound, then withdrew it hastily. "I've been bloody lucky, all round."

"You have. It's one hell of a scar." Paul traced a line across and down Nicholas's leg. "Now at least we're equal." He slid down the bed, to kiss the gnarled and reddened flesh.

"You don't need to do that." Echoes of words he'd used with Phillip. Was the man always going to hover about their bed, salting the atmosphere with memories or comparisons? Nicholas ploughed on, trying to ignore the ghost. "Not for me."

"Don't be daft. I want to. This is a mark of honour and I want to pay it due reverence." Paul kissed the marred skin again, gently, reverently, almost in awe.

"If I'd known it would make so much of an impression, I'd have got one earlier."

"I wish you had. It would have saved me an awful lot of worrying. And having a heart attack every time I saw the telegram boy, wondering if he was heading for us." Paul drew himself up the bed once more, marking his progress with tiny kisses along his friend's flanks, chest, neck, face. It wouldn't be long before they made love again, considering the rate at which he was getting aroused.

"And there was me worrying that every post would bring notification that you'd married some lucky governess." Nicholas squeezed the hands that now lay on his stomach. "We've lived too long in dust and shadows, Paul. We won't ever be so stupid again, will we?"

"Not now. The defences are down and the wall's been broached." Paul pushed himself up, the lascivious cherub expression once more gracing his face. "Now, what did old Henry V say? Once more into the breach, dear friends? The breach is ready if the assault party is."

"It's been ready for years."

DECEMBER 1918. ST. MICHAEL AND ALL ANGELS' CHURCH, LYNDHURST

Nicholas rose from his knees, gently wiping the dirty soil from his trousers; it was an act that he'd performed many times over the years at his own family's plot. Now he was performing the same duties at the place where all the Taylors had come to rest. Ironic that it was almost on Nicholas's doorstep—he could keep an eye on Phillip and put fresh flowers on his grave until his own time came. The beautiful and surprisingly robust angel who guarded the grave bore a striking resemblance to the person who'd once shared his quarters and his bed. There was a knowing look in the angel's eye, just as there'd been in Phillip's in the bedroom of the little pension where they'd last made love. Nicholas wondered if this memorial had been based on sketches drawn from life and whether the artist had been another of Phillip's lovers. Had he experienced the power of that look first hand?

"Sorry it took so long," Nicholas whispered, addressing the angel under his breath. "It didn't feel right to come until the war was all done and dusted. At least it's over by this Christmas." He drew his coat about him against a biting easterly wind which was whipping over the Forest and making his bad leg ache.

A man came out of the church, waving. As he approached, he smiled, his face lighting up—as it had so often down the years, since they were boys—at the sight of Nicholas. Paul, being discreet and sensible, was keeping his distance, not ready to pay his own respects to someone he'd never known but to whom he—they—both owed so much.

"I won't be long now." Nicholas had done all he needed to do, with his bunch of Christmas roses and early winter jasmine. And his few, not terribly coherent, words.

"Take all the time you want. I'll wait down by the lych gate." Paul pointed airily along the sloping path towards the churchyard's entrance. He tipped his head reverently towards the angel, then turned.

"No—you come up here. It's time you at least passed the time of day, even if you'll never meet." Nicholas smiled as his lover picked his way through the dewy grass to the topmost part of the graveyard.

Paul stopped by the grave, stood a moment in thought, then came over and gingerly touched Phillip's headstone. "Old soldiers never die. They live on in someone's memory."

"I'll never forget him. I'm sorry." Whether Nicholas was apologising for the remembrance or his burgeoning tears, even he couldn't tell.

"Why apologise? I wouldn't expect you to forget him." He looked Nicholas in the eye. "You always were an unfathomable sod. I think he knew you as well as anyone could and he wanted the best for you, always. That's how I've always understood his letter."

Nicholas stopped. "Penny for your thoughts?" He'd resolved that, today, he'd ask the question which had gnawed at him so long, "You don't mind that Phillip was first?" But not now, not out here.

"Funny you should say that. Back there," Paul jerked his thumb over his shoulder towards the church, "I sat in one of the pews and had a bit of a think. And a doze— don't laugh, I'm feeling my age and the cold's been getting to my leg, too. I'll tell you all about it over a pair of whiskies, in the local."

Nicholas let himself be led down the path. Paul offered him an arm, which he took gratefully; no one would take a second glance at someone helping along a lame old soldier.

Paul steered them towards the nearest pub, concern written on his handsome face. He wouldn't elaborate until Nicholas was settled into a chair by the fire in the lounge bar and he'd made sure that nobody was within earshot. "Coming here, I had half a mind to go over to his grave and shout him down, for interfering." Paul downed half his drink at once. "But I've decided I should thank him, really, for pushing us together at last. Can't help feeling a bit heartless about it, though. I got you and he got a bullet."

Nicholas smiled. "He wouldn't think that. He'd be the first to shake hands, congratulate you on your luck and offer you a pint, if he was here."

"He was a paragon, then. Unless you're having me on to make me feel less guilty."

`"Not a paragon, a pragmatist." Nicholas looked up, but Paul was smiling. "And you know I can't lie. Never could, to you."

"Can't lie? Then you've been bloody good at hiding the truth." Paul picked some fragments of green from his

102

coat, leaves from the flowers they'd left up at the grave. "Phillip would have agreed. You're bloody useless at saying what really matters."

Nicholas knocked back his own drink. "I'll get the next lot." He walked over to the bar, having to steady himself more than usual on his stick. The cold? The shock of realising he'd have to tell Paul the whole truth? He could barely carry the drinks back safely to their corner.

"Easy there." Paul took the glasses. "You look like you need this." He passed Nicholas his whisky, but neither of them drank.

"I don't think I've lied to you about *him*. I've just omitted too much of the truth." Nicholas sighed, closing his eyes as he spoke the treacherous words. "We were lovers. That time we went trout fishing, then again in France, on leave. He didn't love me—there was another chap, Fergal. They'd argued. That was why he asked me to go fishing with him." Nicholas opened his eyes, ashamed at his own inability to tell a coherent story.

"I see. Yes. Carry on." Paul's voice was soft, his face kind, showing no sign of shock or disappointment, just a growing understanding.

"Fergal was killed at sea. We were on a spot of leave and Phillip was sad. We had a bit too much to drink." Nicholas took a draught of whisky, the fierce burning in his throat a reminder of that intoxicating French wine. "I feel grateful to him, for opening both our eyes, but it's gratitude tinged with guilt. Guilt towards both of you."

"If I'd had the sense to speak sooner, back in 1914, then you'd have cause for remorse on my part. But I

103

didn't and you haven't." Paul cuffed his friend's shoulder. "Did you love him?"

Nicholas looked long and hard out of the window, along the road to the lych gate and the little path up to Paul's grave, then equally long at his friend. "I thought so, once. Now I suspect I only loved the shadow of you I saw in him—you might have passed for cousins, you know."

"I guessed that from the marble angel, assuming that's supposed to be him. Well, if the family hailed from here, maybe there's a by—blow involved somewhere on my side." Paul ran his hands through his dark hair.

Nicholas smiled. "Whatever else Phillip was, he was my friend and I'll always feel indebted to him." He passed his hands over his eyes. "I don't think that sensation will ever pass."

"Maybe it's right that it shouldn't. Keep us grateful and all that." Paul finished his whisky. "I'll try not to feel I got you by default, but I can't help feel conscious of my luck. And his misfortune." He gently touched Nicholas's arm. "I don't know if I've always been first or if I'll always be second to him, but it doesn't matter. Never will matter."

"That's sounds just the sort of thing he'd have said." Nicholas finished his drink and eased himself from his chair.

Paul rose, slipping on his coat and winding on his scarf against the cold. "Maybe he's up there, looking down on us."

Nicholas remembered sunny days, trout for dinner and Phillip's extraordinary dream—all of them now recalled with pleasure and not tinged with remorse. "Maybe, Paul. Maybe."

Hallowed Ground

There was me, the padre and a packet of Black Cats. And bugger all else except the pitch dark night. Me, the padre and a packet of Black Cats we didn't dare light any of, because the Germans might have spotted the glow and that would have been that.

I wasn't even supposed to be there, but I guess neither of us were. He'd been out to take church parade for the lads and wanted to return to base so he could do the same for another poor group of sods the next day. I'd given him a lift from the casualty clearing station, and we were both heading back, when a shell took a fancy to the piece of ground just to the left of us, the little strip we'd played cricket on just two weeks previously, before the Germans moved further forward. Up went me, the padre, the car and all, including Stevens, the poor injured lad we were taking back with us. The lad who was at present scattered all over the field, with his legs at third slip and his head lolling around square leg, if you follow me.

The padre was pretty cut up about it: he'd not long been in France and nothing he'd heard or read had prepared him for the reality of modern war. He wanted to bury Stevens there and then but he'd have ended up getting the three of us buried.

I got him settled into an old shell hole. At least, I got his body settled, because his mind took a bit longer. He kept saying that Stevens would have survived if we'd stayed put, but that was just the shock talking. I know that; I'm a doctor. That's how I also know that Stevens would have had no chance if we hadn't moved him and a pretty slim one even if we'd got him back. That's why we'd taken the shorter way – my decision – because time was one thing Stevens didn't have. I got that through to the padre eventually, but he was still uneasy. Maybe he was guilty that he'd survived and Stevens hadn't. It happens.

Me, the padre and the Black Cats. Until I noticed my pack, which by some miracle had been thrown through the air and landed – pretty well intact – about twenty feet from where we were. I reckoned I could crawl over and get it, so long as I stayed quiet. There didn't seem to be any of the enemy out on night patrol, but the padre wouldn't have it.

"It's not worth the risk," he said, "whatever's in there."

"You might not think that come the middle of the night when you'd be grateful for a wee drop from my hip flask. Think of it as medicinal," I added, because you never know with these clergy types. Some of them seem to think Jesus turned the water into wine so everybody could wash in it. "I've got some chocolate creams, too."

That seemed to settle the matter, although halfway across those twenty feet – which felt like a hundred yards – hearing a nearby crump made me wonder if I shouldn't have argued. Although I suppose if your number's going to come up it can happen as easily in a hole as in the open. I kept going, grabbed the bag and headed back. The look of relief on the padre's face, seen by a Very light's timely illumination, was a picture. You'd have thought I was the Archangel Michael himself, come to bear him up to safety on a fiery chariot or something.

I got myself comfortable again, comfortable being a bit of a loose term given the circumstances, and broke out a bit of the chocolate. The rest would have to be rationed out. He had a canteen of water and we both had our greatcoats, so all in all it wasn't so bad. Stevens would have been glad to swap his conditions for ours. I remembered the padre had mentioned playing a bit of cricket, and thought it might help him if we chatted about it. Quietly, of course, although there was plenty of noise to cover our whispers. It turned out we'd played some of the same teams, before the war put an end to all sorts of innocent fun. We'd faced some of the same bowlers, been smote hip and thigh by them. I was proud of that joke, and he'd laughed at it, but not even talking sport was helping him keep calm.

I suggested we try to get a wink of sleep, because it wasn't going to make a scrap of difference to whether we survived the night, although I didn't tell the padre the last bit. I doubt he'd spent the night under fire before.

The shells kept falling, on and off. Now closer, now further away. And while I managed to grab a bit of sleep in between them – I've always had the ability to drop off at will – the padre was as stiff as a board. In my profession, you get to see plenty of men at the extremity of their life, men who want to find some solace before they go to their long home. It's not quite the absolution of the confessional, divesting themselves of a secret they've carried a long while. You get to recognise the look they wear. The padre must have known that look, too, from his profession. I wondered if he also knew he had it plastered all over his face then and whether he was hoping I'd take the hint.

"If you can't sleep, at least try to relax," I whispered. "It'll be a long time till dawn and it'll go no faster if we worry ourselves through it. Have faith." I hoped he could see my grin, especially if he thought his number had come up. What was it he wanted to get off his chest?

"I have faith. I didn't realise how easily frayed it could get under such circumstances." He sounded as if he was trying to be chipper, hiding a deep fear. I'd heard that tone of voice in others, too.

"Nip of whisky help?"

"No. Keep it for when we really are *in extremis*." He managed a laugh with that. "I suppose you're used to this sort of situation?"

"Not exactly. I normally spend the night under some sort of cover." I *had* passed long hours similarly, but I didn't want to admit the fact. He'd have asked questions and it didn't make for an edifying tale.

He was quiet for a while, and I almost dozed again, but a still, small, unsteady voice, which I bet he never used from the pulpit or lectern, said, "Have you ever had the feeling these will be your last hours?"

"No. Never." It was an honest answer. I'd heard of men being sure they were "for it" and that prophesy coming true the next day, but my belief was that the feeling contributed to the outcome. Maybe if they'd convinced themselves that the end was nigh, they were more reckless in action or something like that. Psychology had never been my strongest suit.

"You're fortunate." I didn't need to ask the padre what was on his mind: his voice made it plain.

"They're nothing to be ashamed of, those thoughts," I said, for want of anything more comforting to say. "And they don't always come true. I know people who think every day is their last." That might have been stretching the truth. "One day they'll be right, I suppose, but they'll have had a miserable time of it up till then."

"Yes. Yes, I suppose it's the worst thing, lacking courage."

"I wouldn't say it's a matter of courage." Not as I'd understood it in the past. "I suspect that the most courageous men are the ones who are most scared, but who still go up that ladder or into that wood, braving the unknown in the cause of duty, despite their misgivings and fears."

The padre chuckled. A nervous, constrained chuckle but one nonetheless. "I seem to have found myself in a shell hole with a philosopher. Who'd have thought it?"

"I'd never have guessed I'd be spending the night with a man of the cloth." I stopped, suddenly agonising over whether I'd invested that joke with any hint of another, more private, more uncomfortable meaning. I hoped he'd take it at face value, although I didn't find out immediately, because an exchange of bullets and a ghastly scream, maybe half a mile away but clear as a bell in a night which had turned deathly quiet, focused our minds on things other than jokes.

"Do you think that was one of the lads at the service?" he asked, eventually.

"It came from the right direction, but there's no way of telling at the moment."

"Yes, of course." His voice had a wavering edge, again. "They all seemed so young."

"Too young," I agreed. No point in trying to deny the obvious. "At least, though, if it was one of them they'd not have died unshriven." Confession, absolution, comfortable words – they'd all been included in the service, which had been surprisingly simple and suitable to the troops' needs. Whatever else was bothering the padre, he should have felt proud of what he'd done for them. I told him so.

"That was just doing my duty, as they do theirs. Nothing particularly special, in the circumstances." He went quiet again for a while, eventually breaking the silence to say, "Do you think it makes such a difference? To die when you've just received absolution?"

That was a whole other debate, to be had with earnest fellow students late at night over cocoa or port. What man or woman ever died in such a state? Who could go from one day's end to the next without making a mess of things somewhere along the line? And in this particular line, it was an hourly occurrence. We didn't exactly offer Fritz the left cheek when he smote us on the right.

But it struck me that his question had seemed more personal than theological, and it needed a personal answer.

"I believe that you have to commit yourself into God's hands and believe His mercy's greater than we'd be inclined to dish out, were we the COs for the operation."

"I do that every day, believe me. I pray it's enough."

What did he have on his conscience that was worthy of such contrition? I wondered if he might even have murdered somebody, given the sombre tone of his voice. Surely it couldn't be that bad?

"Would it help to talk? I know that a problem shared isn't always a problem halved."

He laughed, bitterly. "Sometimes it's a problem doubled."

"It's your choice." It didn't always help to air one's baggage, but in this case it felt like the right treatment. "I promise I'll regard anything you say as coming under medical confidentiality."

"Does medical confidentiality cover immorality?"

"I expect it does." I had plenty I could have said about immorality – or what people termed immoral.

Had he been committing adultery with the verger's wife?

"Hmm." He must have been mulling things over – you could almost hear the wheels of his mind turning, grinding his emotions small – until another explosion, closer this time, seemed to decide things for him.

"I have these desires." This wasn't the quietly confident, reassuring voice he'd used during the service. "Sinful desires. I don't put them into action, but they gnaw at me." He swallowed hard. "Even now, even here, at the end of all things."

"You don't know if it's the end. It's like young Stevens: only God would know if he'd have survived the journey, anyway." If it were possible for a man to die of despair, the padre sounded as though he was heading in that direction.

"If it were the end, I'd die happier if I could tell you about things. You'll detest me."

"Really? How bad can these temptations be?"

"How bad? The unforgivable sin, perhaps. I want other men. To lie with them."

I had to bite my tongue, the temptation to say, "Is that all?" being so strong.

He continued. "It's terrible enough for any man to be consumed with such desires, but for a man of the cloth ..."

I bit my tongue again. So much I could have said, so much I had to keep in. I wanted to tell him that I understood, that I shared his inclinations, although I didn't feel the burden on me so much. I'd been extremely fortunate in the character – and discretion – of my lovers. I wanted to say that he shouldn't fret so much, that plenty of men, good, decent men, felt as he did, and still kept their faith intact. But that would have sounded platitudinous, if not downright callous. Every man's conscience is his own and makes its own demands.

Yet I had to say something, and fast, or he'd think I was disgusted. I tried, "I've always believed there are worse things a man can feel."

"Really?" He sounded surprised.

"Of course. I fail to see how your desires hurt anyone, apart from yourself."

"But you know that scripture says it's wrong."

Scripture. That was a red rag to this particular bull.

"No point in quoting scripture at me if it's any place in the Book previous to Matthew." I tried to keep a civil tongue and a level head. The Old Testament got used too often to defend the indefensible. "These feelings of yours. Do they make you judge where you shouldn't judge, or cast the first stone? Or anything else which is *really* wrong?"

"No, I suppose they don't." The uncertainty in his voice belied his words. "But I can't ignore the traditional teachings. I'm a clergyman."

"Yes, I see that. Caesar's wife should be above suspicion." I remembered a particular clergyman I'd once spent the night with: we'd got as little sleep as the padre and I were having that night although the reasons had been much more enjoyable. *He* hadn't been particularly bothered by Leviticus. "I'm not sure how you've coped, though. It must be hell."

More like hell than even this place was. At least the men were given regular periods of withdrawal from the line and the chance of leave if they survived to enjoy it. You couldn't get a rest from your thoughts and desires; I knew that for myself. It was time for that nip of whisky. I expected him to sip the tot I poured him but he knocked it back like a hardened veteran.

117

He said, "The answer's not in this, I know that from experience, but I do appreciate the comfort it brings. Thank you."

"That's all right." I wished I could offer him some more substantial comfort, but all I had was more whisky – which didn't seem a good idea – and words. "Desires of themselves aren't anything to be ashamed of. Even the Lord was tempted in the wilderness. It's what you do with them that makes the difference."

And even then, there were degrees of difference. I'd never countenance murdering a man in cold blood, but if the Germans were attacking the hospital I'd not think twice about picking up a gun to defend my patients.

"Perhaps," he said, then went quiet again. I shut my eyes, thinking of my lovely young curate who'd lit up the last April bar one. I made sure my greatcoat was drawn close to me, in case my body reacted at the suddenly vivid memory.

Later – half an hour, an hour, two hours, I couldn't tell – the padre said, "Perhaps I should have given in to these desires. Given in, confessed, allowed myself the chance of absolution. Then I wouldn't risk dying not knowing."

"Not knowing what?" I replied, still half stunned from sleep and only realising, as I spoke, how I'd encouraged him onto dangerous ground.

"Not knowing what it would be like to realise those desires. Whether it would be the door to hell or the door to heaven." He shuddered, evidently horrified at his own confession.

I could have given him an honest opinion on that. Whether I had the courage to do so was another thing. Funny how I could face the shelling but was still reluctant to bare my soul, even though we might have been at the end of all things. His shivering helped make up my mind. I put my arm around his shoulders, and drew him closer, a conscious drawing of our bodies together rather than the forced proximity we'd already shared.

"If you want an opinion that's neither medical nor theological," I said, going into action, if only metaphorically, "I'd say that it all depends on the quality of your lover. And whether it means something or whether it's just to scratch an itch. Like the men seem to want to scratch all their itches when they get into town."

He leaned into the hug. "Are you saying that from experience?"

I swallowed hard. No going back now. "I am."

"Would it be impertinent to assume that it's directly relevant experience?"

"It isn't. Rude," I added, just to clarify. "I know the feelings you speak of. The only difference is that I've not fought them. Not since I learned how to give in to them gracefully."

A distant explosion – the first there'd been in a while – punctuated the calm of the night. Perhaps it was going to be the start of a barrage, supposedly clearing the way for a surge forwards at dawn. In which case, I thought, maybe I should offer the padre a chance of eliminating that risk of dying *not knowing*. I supposed you could do it in a shell hole by dark as effectively as in a bedroom with white linen sheets, but I reckoned that would put him off for life.

So I just took his hand in mine: it felt slender, full of sinewy strength.

"If we make it through tonight, remember this. If we make it through the next few months or years or heaven knows what, remember this." I felt the pressure of his fingers on mine. "When this bloody war is over, then please find me. We'll carry on this conversation. I'll give you my honest opinions. You can trust me, I'm a doctor."

A convenient Very light lit up the sky, and the padre's face. I'd never understood what beatific might really mean until I saw his smile, then. He wasn't bad—looking to start with but in that illumination he was beautiful. I couldn't have done anything but kiss him, could I?

He leaned into it, then broke away, his smile rueful now. "Thank you."

"My pleasure." I ran my fingers down his face, along his jaw. "Shame we didn't meet back in Blighty, before this bloody thing blew up."

"I have to disagree." He took my hand again. "I'd have run a mile. This business focuses the mind."

"It does." Time for another nip of that whisky and a bit more chocolate. That was the safest way forward, given that the faint light in the sky couldn't still be the lingering rays of the Very light, and must be the herald of dawn. I raised my flask to make a toast. "Home. Beauty. A clear mind and a clear conscience."

"All four." He drank after me, our fingers touching again on the little flask. "It's a mess, isn't it?"

"A bloody nightmare," I agreed. "Still, it doesn't sound like we're getting a barrage today. Maybe we can even grab a gasper in a while. The sky's brightening."

"I should say Morning Prayer," he said, patting the pocket where he carried his missal.

"We'll say it together. My patients could do with a word put in for them and I wouldn't refuse a bit of comfort, too."

He must have started saying the words mainly from memory, as the light was still a touch too dim to read by. I joined in where I could, the familiar words even more applicable given our situation.

O Lord, our heavenly Father, Almighty and everlasting God, who hast safely brought us to the beginning of this day: Defend us in the same with thy mighty power; and grant that this day we fall into no sin, neither run into any kind of danger; but that all our doings may be ordered by thy governance, to do always that is righteous in thy sight; through Jesus Christ our Lord.

When he reached the end, we sat in silence, sharing the last of the chocolate, until the sound of an approaching vehicle put us back on guard, but it was only one of our lads, sent out to find us. I gave the padre's hand a final squeeze, and a whispered, "When the war's over, find me. Remember?"

"I'll remember."

"We thought you were all gonners, sir," the driver said, as he came to a stop and just remembered to salute.

"Only poor Stevens. They've not beaten me yet," I said, hitching up my pack and waiting as the padre got into the car. "Anyway," I tipped my head in his direction, "I had an advantage. That foxhole was hallowed ground."

The padre looked at me, as if he was about to argue, then broke into a grin. "Hallowed ground indeed."

Music In The Midst

Of Desolation

The Time Was Aeon

Patrick Evans wasn't entirely sure how he'd arrived where he was and he wasn't prepared to ask anyone.

All he could be certain of was that he'd lived twenty—seven years on earth, then been hit by a sniper's bullet in a trench in France while telling one of his company to, "Put out your damned cigarette before Jerry sees it." He'd known he was done for, equally known that he'd only a bit of time to put in order whatever needed to be put in order. He'd prepared for oblivion and then heard Christopher Williams's voice in his head—a voice as lucid as if he was sitting next to the man on a cold winter's afternoon in St. George's chapel, reaching the end of Evensong and anticipating a pre—prandial sherry.

Lighten our darkness we beseech thee, oh Lord and by thy great mercy defend us from all perils and dangers of this night. For the love of thy only son, our saviour, Jesus Christ.

Patrick had spoken the words along with the voice in his head, lying in the mud of Flanders, repeating the collect again and again and—for the first time in his life—actually meaning it. After the fourth repeat he could speak no more. To his surprise, he'd awoken in another place and with another job to do, one a damn sight more pleasant than leading men into a hell of barbed wire and mud.

So Christopher had been right all along about the afterlife being real. Naturally that would turn out to be so; when had Christopher ever been wrong about anything?

Magnificent, beautiful, infuriating Christopher who'd been the unsurpassed source of pleasure in Patrick's life. The one who had sat alongside him on the settee—and on his knee when the rest of the Evans household were out—and played such havoc with his sleep. Night after night for two weeks on one memorable holiday to Trouville, before Europe had been rent apart.

Patrick wasn't sure how long he'd spent *there*, in that other place where time no longer seemed to have the same dimensional qualities he was used to it having on earth. Certainly enough years for the world he'd known to have changed—some said progressed—considerably by the time he returned to it. And now he was on Earth again, on English soil. Only this England had ships in the sky instead of just on the water where they were supposed to be, and cabs were being pulled along by fiercely roaring engines rather than the docile horses God had intended for the job.

If this was progress he wasn't sure he liked it.

Strange Meeting

"You won't be bored, you know." A tweed clad lady of indeterminate age, the person assigned to settle Patrick in on his return to earth, had met him at Waterloo station. She looked more Agatha Christie—he'd seen the author's picture on the cover of a book in WH Smith's store while he'd waited to be scooped up—than any angel he'd ever met. She'd extended a brown, wrinkled hand to be shaken. "Should have introduced myself properly. Call me Marjorie. It's not my name now although it was my name once, and it'll do. Let's get you to your lodgings."

"I've forgotten what boredom's like," Patrick said, barely able to keep up with her, as she set off at a great pace.

Funny how tedium hadn't featured *back there* in the other place, but now a vague memory of what it felt like returned, along with recollections of other feelings he'd left behind. Hurt. Jealousy. Cold. Patrick pulled his jacket tighter around him and wished he was wearing a thicker sweater.

"There's work to be done and they've decided you're suitable to be entrusted with it." The woman stopped in her march, turning to face him and rolling her eyes, as if to insinuate that Raphael or one of his lesser lights was lacking in judgement this time around. "I suppose they know what they're doing."

"What exactly is it that you want me to do?" When he'd first been given his notice to prepare for "embarkation", Patrick had wondered whether he'd be assigned to being Christopher's guardian angel. Any previous occupant of the post would have had to take an extended sabbatical due to extreme mental fatigue. But now he was back on earth, it was obvious the timescale wouldn't work out. According to the newspaper he'd seen at the newsagent's this was 2017, so Christopher—if alive—would be one hundred and twenty—seven and incapable of getting into any mischief that a guardian angel would need to get him out of.

"Do? Be patient in the short term." Marjorie snorted, turning a corner and leading him out of the concourse.

It was odd walking real streets again, even if they barely resembled the ones Patrick remembered. The snow—there'd clearly been a fresh fall during the night—was white or slushy grey, for one thing. Not brown with horse droppings, like it used to be anywhere that cabs and drays plied their trade. It had been speckled brown out in France. Brown and dirty red.

The air was cleaner, too, despite the muck the vehicles threw out. They crossed the river by Westminster Bridge, making their way through the bustle until main roads gave way to a side street and then a labyrinth of residential roads. They ended up in front of a large, neat house with a substantial plot around it, one which didn't seem to have suffered the fate of similar properties they'd passed, redeveloped past recognition. Marjorie had kept up a constant commentary *en route* about what had changed, how the "war to end all wars" had failed to do so and how parts of London had been flattened by a

128

conflict played out over its head that had landed on its doorstep.

Still, in this cul—de—sac, by a white stuccoed Georgian villa, Patrick could believe he was back on leave, newly deposited from a Hansom cab and waiting for the footman to come and take his bags.

"Headquarters. Or, I should say, one of HQ's departments here on earth." Marjorie opened the heavy front door, leading Patrick into a well—kept, elegant hallway. Voices sounded from other rooms, the unmistakable sounds of people, or angels, at work, busy and content. "Come and meet Neville."

She guided Patrick through an open door into a small study, whose French windows gave onto a garden blanketed in snow.

Neville looked entirely like his name had suggested. Big, bluff, quietly efficient. "Ah, Evans." He gave Patrick a vigorous handshake.

"Pleased to meet you." Patrick frowned. "Have we met before?"

"Not directly, although I've seen you on plenty of occasions. I had charge of a friend of yours during the great unpleasantness."

"Guardian angel? That couldn't have been an easy job." And why hadn't there been more of them? Uncomfortable memories of young lads—wounded, dying or simply going mad—calling for their mothers, flooded Patrick's mind.

"It wasn't." Neville sat down, encouraging his visitors to do the same, which was welcome. Back on earth meant back with an earthly body and all the aches and pains that involved. "Easy at the start, nothing more complicated than saving him from stray bullets. Albeit he had a nasty habit of trying to put himself in the way of one." Neville's face broke into an avuncular grin. "Had to make sure he was preserved—as per orders—to see out the war."

"Why weren't they all preserved? Why pick out just one or two for special treatment?" The return to earth had brought a return of anger, too. Patrick didn't ask it for himself—his end had been quick and relatively painless—but for those poor boys.

"Why indeed?" Neville spread his hands. "I could be complacent and say we couldn't have saved them all, not every day for four years. Everyone has to die sometime."

"But the manner of their deaths…" Patrick struggled for words; strange how he hadn't felt this way in so long. How he'd been so grateful to have the sense of injustice flow away. How it had begun to make sense, back *there* and now it made no sense at all.

"Heartbreaking. Yes. And that wasn't only felt here." Neville smiled, eyes burgeoning with tears, tears which were being kept under strict control. "You'll understand one day. Suffice to say that we don't like to intervene, but sometimes we have to. If the…what do they call it, Marjorie? The thing that sometimes goes down the wrong line?"

"Flow chart." Marjorie, voice softer than it had been, sounded as if she too was holding back from crying. "It's a modern thing, Patrick. A sort of map of what might happen if you choose one set of actions or another. Every time someone opts for a particular thing, all the chart lines ahead get reset."

"Sometimes there are key points in the process control system where we have to step in, or else the resetting causes chaos." Neville nodded.

Patrick, who'd just about followed the discussion, wondered what key point had been missed in 1914.

"And if you're wondering whether we ever miss any key points, it's rare." Could Marjorie be reading his mind? "No matter how bad it may seem, sometimes the alternative was worse."

Patrick shivered, despite the warmth of the room. Worse? What could have been worse than hell?

"I think we should return to the matter in hand. Thank you, Neville." Marjorie tapped his arm then smiled benignly at Patrick. "Perhaps you can talk this young man through the general rules and regulations before you give him his specific briefing. No—one better than you for that particular responsibility." She produced what seemed to be an uncharacteristic wink and disappeared. Literally.

"I wish she wouldn't do that. Still gives me a turn when she pops back to HQ in such a theatrical manner." Neville shook his head. "Let me show you where to stow your dunnage, then we'll organise a brew. Briefings are thirsty work."

Patrick was about to question the word "dunnage" when he realised there was something leaning against his leg—a small trunk, like an old—fashioned midshipman's chest, the sort his uncle had possessed when he'd first served in Her Majesty's navy. He had no idea where it had come from but nothing surprised him anymore.

"Yes, it's yours. Bring it up to your quarters."

When they'd climbed the series of staircases, each of them narrower than the previous, they opened the door on a bright room, the snow on the rooftops creating such a brilliance outside there was no need yet for a light. Located high up in the house, this must have been a servant's bedroom once; a favoured servant, given its size, and much more comfortably furnished now than it would have been back then. Neville discretely withdrew, muttering about putting the kettle on, leaving Patrick to unpack the trunk.

Whoever had packed it originally had done a good job—clothes, toiletries, all sorts of necessary items, each one looking like it had been chosen with him in mind, the clothes a perfect fit and of excellent yet unostentatious quality. He'd not needed anything like them this last hundred years but he supposed they were essential now, especially the thicker sweaters. Undoubtedly, he couldn't roam the city in the sort of garments he'd been wearing up until his return to earth. Not if he wanted to avoid, at the least, strange looks and catcalls.

Before he went down to the kitchen he slipped a soft black leather jacket over his pullover, a jacket he'd found folded neatly at the top of the trunk. It fought against the damp cold which had penetrated through to his bones as he'd walked through London. And it spoke of happier days. Christopher had possessed a similar jacket, in deep burnished brown, which he'd worn to go motoring in his infernal automobile. How he would have loved to drive some of the noisy shiny things which had sped—or attempted to speed—past Patrick today.

He blew his nose and went downstairs.

Training

The tea tasted good, as did the cake; honest earthly food was great, if not up to the standards of what he'd been used to at HQ (as he began to think of it now, the expression being the one everybody else used). Patrick found himself having to continually reassess what was going on, because the building resembled less a boarding house than part of a military set up. People had clearly defined roles, there was a sort of coded communication in operation and a quiet efficiency pervaded everything which was going on around him. Not that Patrick was being made privy, yet, to what the set up was supposed to achieve with its "key points".

Neville sat down at the kitchen table opposite him, took a huge swig of his tea, then set about explaining the "domestics". House rules. Where to draw your expenses. How to butter up the quartermaster. *Never forget what you are, but never let on, either. Mum's the word.*

Patrick took it all in, each new instruction helping him to reconnect with what it had been like when he'd still been alive. Maybe much about the world had changed but the fundamentals were no different: people still felt as they always had. They needed to eat and sleep, they laughed and argued and loved. The memories of what each of those things felt like—and so much else—became more vivid.

"Now." Neville poured them both another cup then leaned forwards over the table, something in his demeanour subtly changed.

"Yes?" The timeless ambience of HQ had taught Patrick to be less impatient than he'd been when alive but now he was back on terra firma he was aware of old habits returning. He'd always been one for being up and doing, quick's the word and sharp's the action. Maybe those were the qualities he'd been picked for. To do...whatever it was.

"About your job. Got a good memory or do you need to make notes?" Neville produced a notepad and what was evidently a modern version of a pen.

"Both." Patrick smiled, taking the notepad, but preferring to use the little propelling pencil he'd found in his dunnage. "Belt and braces. Belt in the brain and braces on paper."

It seemed like he'd given the ideal answer. "Excellent. There's a file of information for you, of course, but that's never like your own notes, is it? Right, first thing you need is a name. Billy Byrne."

"B—Y—R—N—E?"

"Spot on. Lieutenant William Byrne, The Countess of Wessex's Regiment, recently returned from Iraq and run down by a lorry first day in civvy street. Ironic, eh?" Neville dunked a biscuit in his tea, consumed it then carried on. "Barely any time to process him at HQ before he was sent back—he's got a job to do down here. Needs a bit of help and you're the man to do it."

"Am I?" Patrick sat up with a start. "You know, I'm still no clearer about what I'm supposed to be doing."

Neville clearly didn't indulge in eye rolling, like Marjorie had done. Instead, he expressed his disappointment by stroking his moustache. "What do they teach you youngsters? Has no—one briefed you at all?"

Patrick shrugged. "Not that I'm aware of. I was simply told to get myself ready and almost the next thing, I was being whisked down here and landed at Waterloo station. Marjorie appeared to scoop me up. Nobody told me why or what was required of me."

"Communication breakdown." Neville shook his head and took consolation in another dunked biscuit. "Happening more and more. Enemy forces at work, I suppose."

Plus ca change? Patrick took another biscuit for himself; this was going to be hungry work.

"Nothing for it but to learn on the job. No other choice, really. Plenty of the lads here will help you along." Neville's clipped tones were somehow reassuring, redolent of bloody good commanding officers Patrick had known. "Different cases, different techniques, same sort of principles."

"I'm sure they'll be very helpful, s…Neville." Patrick stopped himself using the "sir" that came so readily. "Exactly what sort of case will I be dealing with?"

"Like most of the personnel here, you'll be helping out someone who needs something a bit out of the ordinary. Perhaps if you haven't been briefed then you'd better start by reading this." Neville pushed what appeared to be a dossier of information across the table. "I suspect this will keep you occupied much of the rest of the day. Better get up to speed—first rendezvous tomorrow."

Patrick's heart sank. First rendezvous? What did that mean, and however would he be prepared for it? Maybe the answer lay hidden in this great big dossier. He turned over the folder, noted the title "Robert Woodward, c/o William Byrne" and began to read.

The Peril of Love

Billy Byrne had gone straight onto the fast track. Cherry picked in the afterlife just as he'd been when on earth. He'd barely had time to find his feet in HQ, whisked back again almost the minute he'd walked through the pearly gates, then put into Neville's team and told to sit tight and await orders. He was good at that, always had been, and so he'd waited, enjoying the comfortable facilities at the sort of London house he'd only ever seen in BBC dramas. They'd given him little jobs to do, processing data and helping out the quartermaster, but he knew they were just place holders for whatever the real thing was going to turn out to be.

Out in Iraq or Bosnia he'd always had a good grasp of the big picture. Strategy, that was his particular skill. Now he wasn't even sure there was a *canvas*, let alone a picture. Nothing made a lot of sense beyond the obvious, that he'd died, been sent back and was part of some military style operation again, operating behind the scenes rather than in the front line.

When the orders did come, he wasn't too surprised. He was to take up the position of *guardian angel*, *probationer status*, working with another officer. That was logical, it would make reasonable use of his skills, although the identity of the person being guarded was the problem. Never in his wildest nightmares had it occurred to him it would be Robbie Woodward he had to mind.

When Neville briefed him, for the first time in his life Billy found himself questioning a direct order. "Robbie Woodward? Are you sure you've got the name right?"

"No mistake as far as I can see." Neville consulted what looked like a register, tracing the words with his finger. "Yes. Robert Woodward. Born May the third, nineteen eighty..."

"I know when he was born! Sorry." Billy held up his hand in a gesture of apology. "I'm struggling with the idea of having anything to do with him. Assign me to someone else—I really don't mind how difficult it would be. Just not Robbie."

"I'm not sure I have any discretion in the matter. I'm not sure *any* of us do." Neville leaned forward, looking avuncular and reassuring. "What's the problem?"

"Problem? How much time have we got? I suppose you want me to spend all my time making sure he keeps his dick inside his trousers?" Billy immediately regretted the outburst. Neville's expression had turned from avuncular to that of a headmaster addressing the worst behaved pupil in the school.

"I would seek to remind you, Billy, that we don't employ such vulgarity here. Nor would some of the names you've seen fit to use in describing Mr. Woodward in the past be appropriate to our situation." Neville consulted another list, one secreted beneath his register. "*Lecherous bastard. Self—centred sod.* Those are the only ones I can bear to repeat. He will be Mr. Woodward to you, or simply Robbie—is that clear?"

"Yes, sir."

"No need for the 'sir', Neville will do for me." His face softened again. "I'm not unsympathetic. I appreciate how difficult the situation is."

"You already knew about me and Robbie?"

"Of course we did. And I'm delighted you saw fit to admit to both the past association and your misgivings. Couldn't have worked if you'd denied any issues."

Billy nodded, swallowing both his pride and his response. "Will I have to talk to him or do I just hover in the background?"

"I'm afraid there will be instances where you have to make direct contact. I will expect you to be both civil and business—like. Keep your mind on your mission."

"I'll do my best. It would help to know what that mission entails." He'd never gone into action without mapping out everything which could be mapped out.

"That's where one of my colleagues comes in. You'll be working in tandem with him." Neville rose. "He's waiting in the drawing room. You might as well get down to things now."

Billy followed in Neville's wake—it seemed the natural place to be—across the hall and into a large room tucked away at the back of the house. There was a young man waiting there, maybe the same age as Billy had been when he'd died. Presumably he'd cashed in his chips short of thirty, as well. Not what he'd been anticipating, exactly. When Neville had said "colleague" that had raised the expectation of some old buffer along the older man's lines, but Patrick Evans, in black jeans and black leather jacket, had been a surprise.

Nice looking lad, if a touch on the old fashioned side. Not in the cut of that jacket, which was strictly twenty first century, nor in the hairstyle, which was timeless, but in some traditional air about him. Billy decided to dispense with military formalities. He thrust out his hand. "Billy Byrne. Pleased to meet you."

"Patrick Evans." The nice looking lad in the leather jacket had a strong handshake. "We'll be working together."

"I'd better leave you to it." Neville tipped his head towards the hall, saying, "Rumour has it there's a pot of coffee in the kitchen with your names on it. Bring it in here," before leaving them alone.

"Better do as he says. The coffee they make here is better than any I've come across this side of the Atlantic." Billy led the way, unsure if Patrick has been here long enough to get his bearings. Certainly he'd not come across him these last few days.

"I'm not surprised about the coffee. I've only had tea since I arrived but it was the best brew I've ever had." Patrick grabbed a couple of mugs, and a handful of biscuits, while Billy got both the coffee pot and the machine to keep it warm. By the time they'd got back to the drawing room and plugged it in again the smell was too much to resist. Any business would have to wait until they were outside of at least half a cup.

"So you've not been here long?" Billy savoured the aroma before he took his first sip; like good wine, the bouquet had to be enjoyed first.

"Got here earlier today. Been locked away in here reading these." Patrick jerked his thumb at a pile of papers, although he showed no sign of discussing them yet. Maybe the old salts—Billy remembered the required briefings from his own first day—had advised a softly softly approach, the men getting to know each other before they entered into their campaign of action. "You're army, as well?"

"Can you tell from the haircut? Or am I mentioned among those?" Billy took a quick sideways glance at the files on the table.

Patrick grinned. "I'm afraid so. At least, your war record is and...the unfortunate incident with the lorry."

"Bloody hell. Can a man have no secrets, especially when they're so inglorious?" Billy took a deep draught of coffee. "What about you?"

"The Somme. Sniper's bullet. Nothing glorious about it." Patrick studied his mug.

"I've read about the Somme. Seen the old pictures. Must have been a fucking nightmare."

Patrick laid down his coffee, looking the Billy straight in the eye for the first time. "You're the first angel I've heard swear. That's twice now." He grinned.

"That barely counts as swearing. Not down here, anyway. Not now." Billy quickly glanced at the door. "Don't go snitching to Neville. He doesn't like barrack room language."

"I bet he's forgotten more swear words than we've ever learned." Patrick wrinkled his nose. "Yes, it was. A nightmare."

"How much of a pain in the arse would it be for you to tell me about it? I've been fascinated by trench warfare, even when I was a just a nipper. Reading the books and looking at the pictures isn't the same is it? I couldn't ask the books questions."

"Not a pain in the...backside at all. I'm not sure I've ever told anyone about it. Not even Chr..." Patrick stopped, took a deep breath. "No—one."

The Dread of Falling into Naught

An hour over the pot of coffee covered not just the Western front but Billy's own campaign in Iraq. A pair of army careers, one promising and one precociously distinguished, both cut ridiculously short. Billy found Patrick genuinely interesting and it appeared the feeling was reciprocated. If they'd served together they'd probably have forged the ideal partnership of trust and gallantry and it looked like they'd work well together here. Someone, somewhere, knew how to put a company together.

"I suppose we should look at our commission." Billy tried to wrest another few drops from the pot, but only dregs remained, to match the scant crumbs on the table where the biscuits had been. "Rather than gossiping like a pair of old women."

"Nobody would begrudge a pair of old soldiers a chinwag." Patrick pushed his mug aside, flicked away the crumbs and laid out his sheaf of papers. "Now, your— our—assignment. It's to see that Mr. Woodward recovers. Apparently he has work planned for him, important work." Patrick referred to the topmost sheets of paper, flicking through them rapidly. "Not that the exact nature of the work is specified anywhere in this particular file."

Billy restrained the urge to insert some of his more forthright, and alliterative, swear words in between the "Mr." and the "Woodward". "It can't be to do with the army. Robbie's been in civvy street for a couple of years.

He was bloody lucky not to be dishonourably discharged from the tank corps *en route*."

"Is that last bit fact or supposition?"

"As far as I'm concerned it's every fucking word of the truth." Billy stopped, the cold hard look in his fellow officer's—or at least what he now regarded as his fellow officer's—eyes giving him pause. "Sorry, let the heart rule the head, there. Hypothesis."

Patrick smiled. "You're forgiven. I'm not going to say 'don't let it happen again' as I know you won't."

"Too bloody right I won't." He wasn't going to try to like the bastard, though.

"I know he's not exactly your favourite person," Patrick picked up one of his papers then quickly put it back among the rest, "but I'm confident that won't impact on the operation."

Was Patrick a mind reader as well or had the briefing papers been more exhaustive than Billy had anticipated?

"I learned long ago not to let personal prejudices make a scrap of difference to my work. I promise I'll behave if I have to go to the pub with the lecherous bugger." Billy savoured the words, knowing full well there probably wasn't anyone else here he could use them in front of.

Patrick grinned. "You were on your way to seeing Woodward when the lorry hit you. Is that just coincidence?"

Billy narrowed his gaze. "You know it isn't. I bet your bloody dossier tells you exactly what was what. I was on my way to beat the shit out of him. Only your file will say 'beat the living daylights' if Neville's had anything to do with it. I suspect if I'd got there and kicked the bucket on the way back I'd not be *here* now."

Patrick smiled; a frank, rueful smile which spoke volumes about what must be lurking in that file. "What these papers don't tell me is why."

Billy slammed his fist on the table. "Why? Because he deserved it. Robbie Woodward had spent the previous two years—most of which I'd spent on tours of duty or training other poor sods to go out to the Middle East— trying to get my bloke into bed with him. Every time I was posted abroad he was hanging around, taking Rafe down the pub and setting himself up for when there'd be a need for a shoulder to cry on."

"I'm sorry to have to ask you." Patrick looked concerned. "If they'd written it all down in here I wouldn't have needed to..."

"That's okay. You've got to do your job." It still hurt like stink, though. All those do-gooders who said it was therapeutic to talk about things could get stuffed; forcing the words out was only making Billy feel more aggravated. He picked up his empty mug and fiddled with it. "Rafe's a good bloke. He didn't feel the need of filling up the hole in our bed with a great streak of water from the tap."

"I'm sorry?"

"It was a description of Woodward. There's more meat on a butcher's pencil." Billy chuckled, flexing his own, well-honed muscles. Even in the short time he'd been back at HQ, he'd forgotten how good that felt. "Not that Rafe got to savour any of it. Not back then, anyway."

"And now?" They both knew the question had to be asked. Rafe had only a memory to be loyal to now, and the empty space in his and Billy's bed was no longer spoken for.

"I don't know. I don't want to know." Billy's hands tightened around coffee mug, knuckles as white as if it was Woodward's throat he had hold of. "Guess I'm going to find out, though." He laid the mug down before he snapped off the handle. "Anything about it in that bloody dossier?"

Patrick turned over a page, read it through as if to refresh his memory, then carefully closed it. "Not directly. I think that may be the point."

"Meaning?" Billy narrowed his eyes.

Patrick considered for a moment before speaking. "Not sure. Insufficient evidence to make a judgement."

"Insufficient fucking evidence?" Billy shouted. "You can take your insufficient evidence and stick it up…"

The door opened, Neville's head appearing round it. "I said no swearing, Billy, and I meant it. Do try to remember, there's a good lad." The rebuke couldn't have been more weighty if it had itself been accompanied by a barrage of oaths. Neville shut the door quietly behind him.

"Was I that loud or can he hear through walls?"

"Both. I suspect he reads minds, as well." Patrick kept his eyes on the papers. "Billy, do you have a problem with

147

me being in charge of this case? I know that technically you outrank me..."

"You talk about Neville being telepathic. You're doing the same thing."

"I'm not aware of it." Patrick looked up. "But I'm aware of how angry you are—I'd have to be blind and deaf to miss that. If it's all directed at Robbie, we can channel it for the common good. If you're annoyed with the setup then we need to clear the air. Now."

Billy sighed. Guilty as charged. "If they've assigned you as my superior officer than that's what you are. I'll learn to live with it. Maybe it's all for the best—they probably think I'm too hot—headed to take the lead."

"I didn't get the impression, when we were talking, that you were like this when going into action."

"Me? I had the coolest head in the regiment. Couldn't do anything about Robbie Woodward when I was up to my ar...backside in sand. Had to trust Rafe. I was right to."

"He's taking it badly. Your Rafe."

That really didn't help. It was hard enough to think of the love of your life being torn apart by grief, even if you knew that sadness would pass and at some point he'd be made anew with every tear wiped from his eye. "Then why couldn't I have been his guardian angel or something useful?" Even Patrick, or Neville, or some other uber-competent angelic being, couldn't live up to Billy's demanding standards.

"Don't know. Maybe they felt you'd lack objectivity?"

Too right he would. Maybe they, whoever made these decisions, had a point. Still, it was too bloody cruel to have to fuss over the man who'd tried to tup your ewe lamb. "I always knew he would take it hard." The unsteadiness in his own voice surprised him.

"I think I should visit him. It wouldn't be right for you to, just yet. There's always the risk—not just of feelings getting in the way—but of being recognised."

Of course.

There wasn't a risk of immediate physical recognition, and the poor beholder then dropping down dead from shock. The mirror told Billy how much he'd changed from his previous time on earth. *Like looking at my own great grandson*, Neville had put it, and he couldn't think of anything more apt. But there was a chance that very slight resemblance would trigger memories. Add to that the fact they couldn't hide the essence of their personalities—those hadn't changed—and you had the makings of a disaster.

"So if you're visiting Rafe, I'm off to see Robbie?"

"Do try looking like I'm not sending you out on a suicide mission." Patrick spoke with authority, as he must have spoken when ordering his men over the top. "You need to find out what his intentions are."

"I know what his bloody intentions are. *Robbie bloody*—sorry—*him I can't call by an insulting name* only ever had one thing in mind as far as I was aware." Billy turned towards the window, watching the breeze shake powdery snow from the London plane trees. "I suppose I've got no choice?"

"Not that I can see."

"Right." Billy took a deep breath and drew himself up to his full height. No time for cowardice; what would his men have said to see the state he was in now? "I'll do my bit. You see Rafe and find out what you can, then tell me everything before I see Robbie. *Everything*. No pussy footing."

"That's what you want? Whatever the blow, it's not to be softened?" Patrick smiled, holding out his hand. "Shake on it?"

Billy shook his hand. "Gentleman's honour."

The City Lights

Patrick had always liked visiting the city, the country boy marvelling at the sights and experiencing the hustle and bustle, but he wasn't sure whether he liked the twenty first century version. Maybe the air was cleaner, maybe there was less horse muck on the streets, but the sheer weight of ill—mannered humanity depressed him.

He strolled across one of the less well—frequented parks, admiring the waterfowl and their knock—kneed attempts to negotiate ice and snow, then made his way to Rafe Whittaker's offices. He'd an official appointment— Neville's team had extraordinary and unexpected skills in arranging such things—to discuss "The Quality of Welfare Provisions for Bereaved Partners of Military Personnel". He'd even got an impressive looking official pass to produce as guarantee of his authenticity, if the original letter's House of Commons headed notepaper hadn't worked its magic.

Patrick was expected, the elegant young lady at reception handing him over to an even more elegant secretary, who coolly checked his ID before taking him into Rafe's office and handing him over, with a protective air, to the man himself, who welcomed him warmly.

Rafe wasn't quite what Patrick had anticipated. He'd built up, for no other reason than the way Billy had spoken of him and the pen portrait in the file, a mental image of a small, tubby chap, with floppy blond hair and a quiet voice. What he got was someone built like a greyhound, the epitome of the tall dark and extremely

151

handsome man—just Patrick's type, when he'd been here first time around. No wonder Billy had been smitten, and at first sight to boot, if all he'd told him over a bottle of beer (post briefing) had been true.

Rafe's office was impressive, too; he was clearly what Patrick's mother used to call "a catch", the sort of man she'd steer his sister in the direction of. Polite, intelligent, astute and—Roger had begun to appreciate just how much angels knew about these sorts of things—hurting very deeply. Desolation, grief, anger, bitterness with the army and the war, all those emotions played subtly in Rafe's voice and words, even when he and Patrick were just passing initial pleasantries. The wound of sudden bereavement ran deep.

"Have you worked for Morkel and Steyn long?" Patrick was about to add some small talk about being sure the company had existed in his days, that his father had used their legal services, but remembered just in time where he was and, more importantly, what year the calendar displayed.

"Since I left university. They're a good company, if a bit on the old fashioned side." Rafe ushered his guest to a chair. "Nothing wrong with that, though. There's a place for corporate morality, even if some of my contemporaries think that's outdated."

"I'm pleased to hear it. There's nothing outdated about decency." *Stop flirting.* Patrick took a deep breath. Rafe was damned attractive but any sort of flirtation would be wrong on about a dozen different points. "You clearly enjoy your work."

"I do. Even if my mother says I should be doing something a bit more...useful. *You should be working for a charity. Or finding some other way of serving humanity, dear.*" Rafe produced what was clearly an impression of Mrs. Whittaker's high pitched tones. "Although look at where serving humanity got Billy."

Patrick resisted pointing out that Billy had been killed by a lorry on the way to inflicting bodily harm on a love rival, rather than by a grenade on the road to Baghdad. Grief tended to rob people of their powers of logic. "You don't agree with her?"

"Not at the moment. I mean, it might be right one day but it isn't now. This is." Rafe tapped the papers on his desk. "You wanted to talk about how I'm coping? I'm fine." The drawn look on his face belied his words.

"I have a confidential survey I'd like you to complete, about how you feel you've been treated. Up to and including my visit." Patrick handed over an impressive looking form, another of Neville's little gems. "If you could fill it in when I've gone and then post it, I'd be grateful, but don't feel under any obligation."

Rafe flicked through the form. "If this is all it's about, then why make an appointment?"

Patrick had anticipated the question. "We make sure we visit a proportion of our clients," strange word, although Billy had insisted it would sound right, "in person. You can't ask a form questions." He smiled, pleased to see the answer appeared to satisfy Rafe.

"If you want questions, I've got a few. Like what happened to the rest of Billy's personal effects. The ones he didn't bring home on leave." Rafe fingered his cuffs, nervously. "I've not had everything back I should have, and it hasn't gone to his father."

"I've been asked to apologise about that. Hit a wall of unnecessary red tape, I'm afraid. We'll see that they're all returned to you. If you still want them." It was a promise Patrick could make with confidence, as Neville had the things bundled up and ready to have delivered.

"Still want them? Do you think I'd change my mind after weeks of trying to get my hands on the bloody things and being fobbed off with some fucking nonsense about the official secrets act? He wasn't in the SAS or anything." Rafe ran his hands through his hair. Thin lines were showing around his eyes, although he could have hardly been more than thirty. Strain, rather than age, seemed to be the culprit. "I don't have a lot else to remember him by. Travelled light, our Billy."

Patrick wondered how Neville had manoeuvred around all the red tape and got his paws on the stuff, although he'd learned within the first few hours at the house that it didn't do to ask too many questions. *On a need to know basis, young man, you need to know only the bare minimum at present*, had been Neville's watchwords.

The arrival of a secretary with a pot of coffee and a plate of biscuits changed Rafe's demeanour. He smiled, thanked her politely and offered his guest a cup.

"Just a small one," Patrick thought he might end up floating at any moment, not on wings but on continual caffeine consumption. When you'd been used to the

Camp coffee brand, drinking a full roast, or whatever they called it, was a shock to the system.

"Are you ex—services?" Rafe offered the biscuits.

"No, thanks. And yes. Yes to the services bit."

"You can always tell." There was something like pride in Rafe's words, pride at a lover who'd served his country well, who'd made more of his life than other men who'd lived twice or three times as long. "Squaddies might as well have the word tattooed on their foreheads." He grinned, but there was no longer any bitterness in it, not regarding Patrick, anyway. For all that he might have plenty to say against the army, Rafe clearly had plenty of time for the men it employed.

"Old soldiers. They may fade away, but they never lose that aura." It was true. You could see it even after they were dead, in Neville and his band of cronies. Marjorie was ex—WRAC as well. "Do you keep in touch with anyone out of Billy's regiment?"

Rafe shook his head. "I've no reason to. Some of them were Billy's mates, even back here when he could choose who he hung around with, but they were never mine. There's just one other pal of ours who I still meet up with but he's ex—tanks. He tells me a damn sight more about what life's like out there," Rafe didn't need to be any more specific about where "there" was, "than Billy ever did. At last I'm starting to understand a bit about what he must have lived through. And how lucky he was not to have died ages ago."

Tank corps. Patrick could have a pretty good guess at this mate's name. "You need good friends beside you, real friends, at a time like this."

"It's certainly when you find out who your real friends are. Funny how many people can't bear to even have a drink with you anymore." Rafe let out a long breath, like a man having thought hard and now coming to a conclusion. "I feel a bit of a traitor, though. Billy wasn't keen on Robbie. Thought the bloke was a gob mouth. Only Billy used a different word instead of mouth." He stopped, eyes narrowed. "I'm not sure why I'm playing at bleeding heart all of a sudden. You *are* from the MOD, aren't you?"

"Why else would I be here? Anyway, I'm not smart enough to fake my credentials." Even if Neville was. "Your reaction's par for the course. The girls in the department say I have a sympathetic manner. I need it—and a pocket full of clean hankies."

"Do you often end up with women weeping on your shoulder?" Rafe almost smiled, for the first time since they'd met. "I'm not surprised. You're a good looking bloke. And yes, sympathetic. Bet you don't have that many grieving men to deal with, though."

"You'd be surprised. This is the twentieth..." Patrick corrected himself, "Twenty—first century, after all. We're supposed to be gender and orientation blind or whatever the fancy term is." He fetched a handkerchief from his pocket. "Want to lay in supplies, just in case?"

"No." Rafe laughed, his handsome face crinkling into those fine lines again, giving him the distinction that Billy had already spoken of. He must have adored the bloke. "I've cried on Robbie's shoulder often enough, so I won't go soaking your lapels. I'm probably not your type, anyway. A colonel's daughter with a passion for show—jumping would be more in your line."

"Is this Robbie your type?" Patrick regretted saying it as soon as the words were out. "Sorry, I…"

"Cheeky bugger." Rafe laughed again. "No, you're all right. I can't answer the question because I don't know. He's a good mate. Might be more than that one day. Might not."

Patrick nodded. It had been the same with Christopher, long ago, before they'd been brave enough to tackle the dangerous corner in their relationship and come round it lovers rather than friends. He didn't have to look further than Rafe's eyes for the truth of the answer, the windows to his soul showing up all his doubts and guilt. "Now, back to the boring stuff. We need to sort out the last few bits of paperwork…" he produced some more official looking forms and they turned their minds to matters mostly administrative.

When they'd finished, Rafe showed Patrick to the door himself, not leaving it to his secretary as he most likely did with other visitors. "When will Billy's things come?" They dithered on the front steps, despite the cold.

"Within three days. If they don't, ring the number I left you and create merry hell." It was Neville's direct line and he'd make sure matters got progressed.

"Thank you. I'm sorry I can't offer you a pint in return for all you've done, but I've got a conference call over lunchtime." Rafe tipped his head to one side, just like Christopher used to do. Patrick pretended he had to check the catch on his briefcase. "And tonight it's my twice weekly pie and pint with Robbie. Robbie from the tanks."

"Don't worry. I'm not supposed to fraternise with clients." Patrick looked up, having composed himself at last. "Have a nice evening."

They shook hands, Patrick striding away down the street puzzled at the strength of his feelings. As he turned at the corner, he glanced back; Rafe was still there, standing on the steps, looking small and lost.

Winter Song

"Is that all?" Billy's face wore such a look of relief that Patrick had to swallow hard. This conversation wasn't going to be easy, even over the finest sandwiches and soup that Neville's team had been able to rustle up. "Rafe and Robbie meet up twice a week for a pie and a pint?"

"That seems to be the sum of it." Patrick had decided not to mention the "crying on his shoulder" bit just yet.

"They sometimes go to the rugby, too." Patrick consulted his notes. "The Harlequins." That had somehow emerged during the filling in of forms, an incoming phone call about tickets for a cup game creating the need for apologies and explanation.

"Oh, great. That was *our* treat, watching the rugby." The look of relief had slipped a bit.

"As far as I can tell," Patrick had been able to tell quite a lot, angels always able to hear more than the words which were spoken to them, "they've not gone further than what we used to call a manly embrace. Crying on the shoulder," he was pleased to slip that in without further comment, "but not sharing pillow talk."

"Thank God for that." Billy ran his hands through his hair. "I went out this morning and tracked down one of Robbie's mates—luckily he hadn't changed his barber. Had to have the Barnet cut in the process, but at least he gave me the same impression. Nothing doing. But not from want of trying," he added.

"How did you wangle that out of him?" It wasn't the sort of thing Patrick used to talk about at the barber's and he wasn't sure the world had changed *that* much.

Billy grinned. "It's the sort of place with a particular clientele, if you get my drift, so turning the conversation to good—looking blokes is almost obligatory. I said he was a friend of a friend."

"Rafe said something odd." Patrick consulted his notes again, more to keep from making eye contact than anything else. "He said he was trying to get tickets for some big game, but he was worried about how Robbie would cope in a really big crowd. He said he's got PTSD. What's that?"

"Doesn't it say in your notes?" Billy's voice, suddenly clipped and tense, made Patrick look up again. The man was pale, as drawn as Rafe had been.

"Would I be asking you, if it did?"

"It's something called post—traumatic stress disorder. A bit like what you might have called shell shock or, what was the other word? Neuro..."

"Neurasthenia."

"That's the one. Nasty, if you've really got it and aren't just malingering."

"Then it's exactly like neurasthenia." Patrick's voice had gone quiet.

Billy wished the ground would swallow him up—or better still, Marjorie swoop down and take him back to HQ. He'd never been particularly subtle and whatever delicacy he'd possessed seemed to be deserting him. "Bloody hell, foot in mouth time again. I'm sorry, Patrick. I

160

didn't mean to cast aspersions on you or your men. Only on Robbie."

"You think he's malingering?"

"Or overegging the pudding to get Rafe's sympathy. PTSD? How the hell is he supposed to have got that?" He left the bit about "if it's real" to mutter under his breath. Anybody should be given the benefit of the doubt; anybody but Robbie Woodward.

"It was as a result of serving in Afghanistan. And before you say anything," Patrick raised his hand against any argument, "I checked his record. Neville got into the official files and I double checked with HQ. *The* HQ. His war record was exemplary, both on paper and as a matter of fact, as observed by...well whoever observes and records these things."

"Maybe they recorded it wrong." Billy forgot to keep the statement under his breath this time. "That's not what I heard."

"You heard wrong. Or maybe you heard what you wanted to hear. As far as I can see—and as far as *Neville* can see if you don't trust my judgment—Robbie Woodward was a good soldier, a real hero. I'd have wanted him in my corps."

Somewhere outside a blackbird was singing its heart out from a tree, despite the cold. Billy had read somewhere that it raised the men's spirits to hear birdsong out in the muddy hell of France. The sound didn't seem to be working its magic now. "I'm not doubting your judgement."

161

"Good, because if you don't trust me then there's probably not a lot of point in our working together. He's not a bad bloke."

"But you don't know him like I do. Did." Billy was about to trot out all the arguments he'd been rehearsing since the day before, but the look in Patrick's eye stopped him in his tracks.

"There's only one way to settle this. Go and find out for yourself. Not from him, because you won't believe a word he says. Talk to his mates, any of his old colleagues you can track down. There are some contact details here." Patrick tapped the files—had this eventuality been already foreseen by Neville, or whoever had put the stuff together? If so, they must have known how much Billy hated the man. "Only be quick about it. Time's a commodity that's on short commons down here."

Billy grabbed the papers, flicking through them and quickly finding the relevant sheet. "I'm going right now."

The Chances

It wasn't hard to find the right bar. There'd been one they'd all frequented, down the Old Brompton Road, back in the days before Rafe and Billy were even an item. He'd guessed his old partner wouldn't be entertaining Robbie there—Rafe had gone upmarket a long time ago. Anyway, this place would have held too many memories, surely? There was the alleyway down the side of the club, just as dingy as it had been when he and Rafe had shared their first kiss and a bit of a grope, both just a little worse for wear.

Funny how some of the old crowd couldn't break the habit, though. He could see two of them through the window, propping up the same places on the bar they were propping up five years ago. Easy enough to go over and strike up a conversation. They'd not known him well enough to sniff out some hint of recognition and if he used an assumed name nobody would be any the wiser.

As it was, it only took about a pint and a half to turn the topic to the army, given that the evening paper on the bar carried a story about the latest casualties. Billy thanked God he hadn't recognised the names, because he wasn't sure he'd have been able to cover up his shock.

"Some of *our lot* fight out there." Simon Youngs had always got maudlin over his evening pint or two, and old habits clearly died hard. "Don't Ask Don't Tell my arse. British Army's always had gay blokes in it and they've been bloody good soldiers. *They* know what it's really like for the lads. Look at Owen, look at Sassoon."

163

Billy had forgotten Simon's other tendency, to spout war poetry at the slightest provocation. Everyone present listened indulgently to his rendition of *Dulce et Decorum Est*; maybe Patrick should have been here to tell him what he thought of the stuff.

"The old lie? Hasn't changed in a hundred years, has it?" Billy had to force the words out, suitable to the occasion if not to his own opinion. He'd have been proud to die for his country, protecting civilians in Iraq, or wherever he was needed, killed by a lorry carrying a suicide bomber rather than one in the middle of London laden with nothing more dangerous than a load of cheap shoes and a driver who'd had a heart attack at the wheel.

"Just as well Billy isn't around anymore to hear you say that." Simon wagged his finger. "He'd have knocked your block off. Very proud of the army, he was."

Billy was saved from having to make an immediate reply—just as well, as he hadn't been prepared for this and it had been a hell of a shock—by Simon's friend Dave feeling the need to explain.

"It's like this...sorry, did we get your name?"

"Robin." Billy immediately regretted the choice, because it was a name he hated, but it was all he managed to blurt out.

"You see Robin, Simon had this pal called Billy. He was a lieutenant in the Countess of Wessex's regiment. Bloody good soldier."

"You knew him well?"

"Not really, just on nodding terms, but I've heard a lot about him. A real hero."

"Did he die on active service?" Billy wondered how close the reply he got would be to the truth.

"That's the irony. He died about a mile from here, knocked over on a street corner."

Billy fought to contain the anger he still felt about his seemingly pointless death. "Doesn't sound that heroic. I suppose he saved the knight in shining armour bit for when he was in uniform? Hey, steady!" Simon had shot off his barstool to grab Billy by the lapels. He pushed him back before it got to a fight, one in which there could only ever be one winner, angel or not. Simon seemed to be getting ready to take the matter outside, although Dave restrained him.

"Don't you insult our Billy," Simon yelled. "He threw himself in front of that lorry to save this woman and her little girl. If he hadn't taken the brunt of the impact, they'd have been history."

"I'm sorry, I didn't know." He genuinely didn't. He'd been too angry to notice anything around him at the time, intent on one thing only—going and kicking Robbie Woodward's head in. Yes, there'd been a little girl, maybe four or five years old, in a green jumper and shorts, but he hadn't deliberately sacrificed himself for her or anyone else.

"It was all over the papers. I'm surprised you didn't see it." Simon was getting a grip again.

"I've been away, so I'm not up with the news." Billy held out his hand. "My fault. Sorry."

"Enough said." Simon shook the hand he was offered. "Billy wouldn't have held a grudge, so I won't, either."

Wouldn't he? How little you knew me. "He was a better man than most of us, then. Did he leave any family behind?"

"His dad was a widower, but I don't know much about him apart from that. Billy didn't speak about family. There's his partner, of course. Rafe." Simon nodded. "He's really cut up about it."

"Are you king of the bleeding obvious?" Dave rolled his eyes. "Of course he's cut up. I heard he was so desolate he'd thought about jumping in front of a lorry himself."

"That bad?" Billy swallowed hard at the thought of Rafe—his Rafe, so full of life and optimism—being driven to such ideas. God, he must have been low.

"Worse than I'd thought it possible. If it hadn't been for Robbie, I suspect Rafe would have launched himself off Westminster Bridge." Simon glanced at Dave. "And I'm not being overdramatic, am I?"

"For once, not."

An exchange of banter and fond glances gave Billy the chance to regather his thoughts. Robbie. Well, the name had cropped up at last. "A bloke needs good friends at times like this." He forced the words "good friend" out, hoping his discomfort wasn't too evident.

Simon took the platitude at face value. "Yeah. And Robbie's a diamond geezer."

Diamond? Pain in the arse, yes, but never a diamond. "Chances are he'll become more than just a friend at some point? Stands to reason, doesn't it, if he's doing the consoling." Billy hoped he didn't sound as hostile as he felt.

"Maybe one day," Simon said, although he didn't appear convinced. "Not yet. It's all too raw."

Billy hid his grin of delight by finishing off his beer. "What did Rafe think of his boyfriend being such a hero? My mum used to say that sort of thing helps with the grief but I'm never sure." That didn't sound a very convincing load of waffle, either. Why couldn't he be allowed just to go and ask Rafe direct? Just to see the pride or anger or whatever emotion was going to show on his face. Just to see his face again...

"He was proud as punch, in an odd way. Said it was just the stupid bloody thing the silly sod would have done. That's his words, not mine," Simon added.

Billy resisted saying, "I bet they were. He never overegged the pudding."

"Didn't stop him being upset, though," Dave observed. "Maybe it made it worse."

"Why's that?"

"Something he said in here, when he was drowning his sorrows, the day after Billy's funeral." Dave called the barman over to refill their glasses.

"I'll pass, thanks all the same. This one's on me, though." Billy had his money on the bar before anyone could argue. "What did he say?" He tried to sound casual, as if this wasn't one of the most important questions he'd ever asked.

"He was going on about how Billy had been so brave, going out and fighting while he sat in a solicitors' office

167

thumbing through papers and helping fat cats in grey suits. How it was all bloody useless."

"He never…did?" Billy corrected himself, avoiding the words, "He never helped any fat cats if he could help it. Quite the opposite."

"It was just the grief talking, I guess, but he seemed pretty depressed about it. Said he felt like he'd let Billy down, somehow, because *he* couldn't ever do anything so important." Simon looked into his beer, like he might find all the answers to life's mysteries hidden in it. "I think he just missed him like buggery. Big empty hole in his heart and his life."

"And this Robbie came along and plugged it?" Billy had to ask it, like a kid picking at a scar. It didn't matter that it kept hurting, that it simply made the process of healing last even longer.

"Like I said, as a friend." Simon's eyes narrowed. "What's it to you? Got your eyes on Rafe yourself? I'll have to warn you, you're not really his type, even if he was ready to go paddling paws again."

"Maybe it's Robbie I've got my eye on." Billy made a show of looking at his watch. "Right. Places to be. Nice to meet you, lads. Don't forget it's your shout next time."

"You'll find us here most nights. Catch us on a Wednesday and Robbie might be here. He'd eat you with a spoon."

Not if Billy managed to whack him over the head with it first.

The Letter

Patrick had been watching for Billy's return. He should have had absolute trust in his colleague but part of him wasn't convinced that Billy wouldn't be haring round to Robbie's to belt the bloke one. Especially if the answers he got at the bar were too provocative. So it was a relief to see Billy striding purposefully along the street, even if he had a face like thunder.

Perhaps he should get the kettle on again.

By the time he'd got Billy settled in a chair with a large, steaming mug, Patrick felt it was safe to ask the vital questions. "Are things any clearer now?"

"Clear as day. I've had a bit of a shock, though." Billy cradled his mug with tense hands, knuckles almost bursting though his skin. "Bloody hell, I sound like a teenage girl. Right, cut the shock bit. I found some information which might affect our plan of action."

"About Robbie?"

"Not directly. About Rafe. He wanted to kill himself and Robbie made sure he didn't." It still clearly cost Billy a lot to say anything nice about his rival. "And apparently, contrary to all we've been told, I died a hero's death. Or so everyone believes down here."

"Care to enlighten me?" Patrick pitched his voice as soft as the breeze. He wasn't unsympathetic. If the roles had been reversed, if Rafe had been Christopher, he'd have felt the same wild horses of emotion tearing him apart.

169

"About the suicidal feelings or the encounter with the lorry?"

"Either. Both."

"It seems I shuffled off this mortal coil while saving a little girl's life. If the lorry hadn't got me it might have got her. Not that I was conscious of any of that at the time." Billy took a large swig of tea.

"Rafe didn't mention it. And it's not in your file." Odd that, on both counts. Rafe could be explained away—if he'd felt suicidal then maybe it was still too painful to discuss Billy's death in detail—but what about the lack of official information?

"It's probably all linked up to whatever it is we're supposed to be doing. Giving me a different perspective on things. At least my death had some good come out of it, even if I'm not sure what good we're doing now." Billy drained the mug, thumping it down on a little table.

"Stopping a key point resetting the wrong way?"

"What?"

"Don't ask me to explain, because I'm not sure I can." Patrick launched into repeating, almost verbatim, what Neville and Marjorie had said.

"A celestial flow chart. Now I've heard it all." Billy sat back, running his hands nervously through his thatch of hair.

"I believe we've been given a role in making sure Rafe makes some vital decision. Like Robbie played a part in making sure he was still around to make it."

After what seemed an age, Billy found his voice. A quiet, almost cracked voice, not his usual confident tones.

"Okay, he's probably got a genuine affection for Rafe, rather than just wanting to get his leg over. Or the nearest the bastard can manage to one," he added, although the insult sounded half—hearted now. He looked at Patrick, who just waited patiently for the inevitable explosion. "Yeah, I know. That's the whole fu...bloody point. I can see they should be helping each other to get well again and we both know exactly how that's going to end. They'll be..." Billy clearly couldn't bring himself to say what they both knew he meant.

Lovers. Doing the horizontal tango.

"And aren't we, you, supposed to be—what's the term I've heard people use—facilitating the process?" Whatever progress had been made by the twenty—first century, the state of the English language had definitely declined. "If they don't get together, then the decision won't be made."

Billy looked up, like a man with one final card to play, one last weapon in the fight. "Why can't Rafe's guardian angel handle it? He's got one, all right—I met the bloke at HQ. He said he was on long distance operations mainly, not 'at the front' but I don't see why I have to do the dirty work and not him. He's not got any vested interest."

"Orders, Billy." It was an irrefutable argument. Two old soldiers knew better than to kick against them. "Somebody's got it all planned out, somebody who knows more than we do." Patrick had to believe that the likes of Neville and his cronies were a damn sight more effective than the strategists of the Great War.

"All right, you win." Billy leaned back again, closing his eyes. "Billy Byrne takes the suicide mission and Christopher Williams gets to put his feet up with the rest of the lads."

The sharp spike of pain and fear shooting up Patrick's spine took him by surprise. He'd not felt any such powerful emotion—physical or mental—since 1916. "What did you say Rafe's guardian was called?"

"Christopher Williams. His number came up in 1940 when he was out fire watching in Stepney and the roof he was on gave way." Billy's eyes narrowed into shrewd slits. "Do you know him? Did you know him?"

"I knew someone with that name, back before I signed up, although it's common enough. May not be the same bloke." Patrick ignored the nauseous feelings in his stomach and throat, the realisation that, given the way everything was turning out, this was bound to be *his* Christopher.

"He'd have been born around the same time as you, I guess. That means nothing, though, does it?"

"No. Shouldn't get our hopes up." Patrick looked down into his empty mug. Billy was bound to notice the inflexion in his voice—why had he gone and given himself away so easily?

"Oh fu...bloody hell, no. You're going to tell me he was your boyfriend or something, aren't you?" Billy rubbed his temples. "Someone's having a right laugh."

Patrick nodded, still keeping his gaze away from Billy's. "For the three years running up to the war." It still hurt, worse than the bullet which had taken him down, and it felt even more painful now he was back on earth. "He meant..." he looked up. Billy would understand, better than anyone else he'd ever spoken to. "He meant everything to me."

"Then I take my hat off to you. I'm not sure if you were braver out in the trenches or back here trying to keep it hidden." Billy smiled, briefly exposing the part of his personality which he must have habitually kept hidden from everyone. Everyone but Rafe. "Bleeding mess, isn't it?"

"Yes." And not just here. If Christopher had been knocking around HQ since 1940, why hadn't he made an effort to find Patrick? He'd already met his mother and father, who'd lived to see a second war encompass the world. And his little brother Henry had appeared almost as soon as he'd been killed, at the height of the Blitz.

Billy punching his fists together snapped Patrick out of his thoughts. "Right. I'm getting Neville in here and asking him what the fu...hell's going on."

Neville didn't need calling for. Maybe the emotional machinations had registered on his radar, or perhaps the almost—swearing had made his hackles rise. Whatever the cause, he strode through the door at a brisk march. "What's all this, then?"

Patrick launched into an efficient précis of their conversation, not least because he couldn't trust Billy not to eff and blind his way through the story. "We've had so many surprises along the way, we just wanted to make sure there wasn't anything else going to come steaming round the corner. We can't make the mission work if you won't be frank with us." It was the nearest he'd ever come to insubordination.

Neville seemed like he was about to explode, looking from one man to the other as if unsure which one he wanted to tear a strip off first. Somewhere in the decision process, the anger transformed into laughter. "Silly sods, the pair of you. How the hell did you think that putting you and Christopher together was going to get the job done, Patrick? No vested interest?" So he *had* overheard them; maybe the room was under surveillance. With the resources on hand in HQ, they wouldn't even need an electronic bugging device. "No vested interest, my aunt Fanny."

"Excuse me?"

"Ask him yourself, Patrick. He'll be here in a few days working the other half of the operation. Only he can't get that up and running until you two clowns have done your part. Once more into the breach, gentlemen." Neville gave a salute and made to leave.

"No." Billy was showing a mutinous streak, too. "With all due respect, Neville, that's not good enough. When we were in HQ we'd forgotten about pain or what a broken heart felt like. But you've conscripted us back here and you're not going to treat us like a pair of mindless squaddies."

"I apologise. Old habits die hard." Neville shook his head. "I know it's a bit of a mess, and if there was another way of working things then I'd have grabbed it. But there isn't—Marjorie and I have looked at all the options and this is the only way we can move things forward. The

174

combination of inside knowledge and impartiality." They stood in silence, all three, listening to a plane passing over, a dog barking in one of the neighbouring gardens, the ticking of the grandfather clock, and Billy's rapid, furious breathing. A stand-off, like watching Fritz across No Man's Land and waiting for the first volley.

Patrick felt he had to break the silence. "Seems like we have no choice," he said with quiet authority. He'd been in this sort of place before, talking his men through another day in the trenches. "If you say we're part of some bigger plan then we have to trust you. Please God that you're right."

Neville laid one powerful hand on Patrick's shoulder and the other—scarred across the knuckles, like a prize—fighter's—on Billy's. "Can I give you my assurance you may be lions but you're not being led by donkeys this time. Neither of you."

Billy seemed to crumple, defeated. "I want to believe you." He picked up the case papers and worried at them, nervously. "I think I do believe you've got your plan all worked out, but it hurts like hell to be on the receiving end. It's not that I'm a miserable bastard—don't you dare get on my case for using that word, Neville—who doesn't want to see his old love have another chance of contentment. I'd do anything to get all the grief and anger out of his system." He looked up. "Anything except getting him into bed with another bloke. That still sticks in my craw, even though Robbie Woodward probably isn't as bad as I thought he was."

"We don't wave magic wands, Billy." Neville's voice was kinder than Patrick had believed possible. "But we can't send you back to Rafe. It'd scare him to death for one thing, given his fragile state, and then where would we be?"

Patrick eased the papers out of Billy's hands, putting them where he couldn't cause any further damage to their already frayed edges. "You've got to be brave, mate. And you've got to be practical. What if this is the only way of getting Rafe to do whatever it is he's supposed to? What if Robbie Woodward's his only chance of finding real happiness again, like he found with you?"

"I know I'm about to spout off like a bloody teenage girl, Patrick, so take the rip out of me as much as you want to." Billy was clearly making his last play and he didn't sound convinced it was going to make a scrap of difference. "I just can't bear sharing him with anyone else."

"You've made that abundantly clear." Neville squeezed Billy's shoulder. "Let Rafe go, old boy."

"I'll look after him." Patrick put his arm around Billy's shoulders, glancing at Neville and then towards the door. The old soldier nodded, slipping out of the room quietly. Anyone looking through the window would have seen what appeared to be simply two men, one of them sobbing his heart out and the other one doing the consoling. Two old soldiers, refusing to fade away.

Patrick waited for the all shaking to stop, and at least some of the anger to calm, before he spoke. "If the situation was reversed, Rafe would have let you go."

Billy rummaged in his pocket for a handkerchief. "Too right. He was always far too considerate for his own good."

Patrick swallowed hard. Time for some home truths. "You said you couldn't share him with *anyone else*. I bet if it really was just anyone else you'd not be putting up half the fight. It's not the principle, it's the *personae dramatis*."

"Dramatis personae." Billy rubbed eyes which were already red and puffy. Strange how the return to earth had brought such an incredible return of all human frailties. "Rafe loved me. Doesn't that count for anything?"

"It did then. And in time to come it might once more," Patrick said, not entirely sure what we meant but knowing he'd got to the crux of things. Would he have been any more dispassionate if Christopher had been involved? Would he hell as like, and Billy would have had to be the one delivering "the talk". "For now, it doesn't appear to amount to tuppence. Sorry."

Billy went over to the window, addressing the panes—maybe he knew how painful it was for Patrick, as well. "I don't believe Rafe loves Robbie. I know they hang out at the rugby and he's relied on the swine more than I'd given credit for, but it isn't the sort of love we had."

"Not yet, it isn't." Patrick didn't move from the spot; Billy might be able to escape eye contact but he couldn't escape the words. "And perhaps not for a while to come, but I think you're trying to fight the inevitable." He let the quiet swamp them again, the gentle sounds of birdsong

177

from the garden, the distant hum of traffic and the space in which to think likely to work better on his comrade than any amount of reasoning might. "They'll fall in love in the end. We need to make sure it doesn't happen too late to count."

A great, shivering sigh coursed down Billy's body. "Right. They win." He spun on his heels. "Plan of action?"

"You tell Robbie Woodward to get his bloody act together and make sure Rafe knows exactly how he feels."

"Just like that."

"*Just* like that. Unless you want to risk the pair of them spending the rest of their lives never saying what they mean, like two characters in some stupid Victorian novel who end up wasting all their chances." Patrick came over to stand by his comrade, looking out at a world they only half connected with. "How brave are you, Billy? You put your life in danger for your country time and again—will you face the same sort of test for Rafe?"

Billy turned, at last, to look Patrick straight in the eye. "Bayonets drawn and over the top?"

"Maybe. In this case the pen may be mightier than the sword."

"Sorry?"

"I've had an idea. We need to find some writing paper and you'd better remember what your handwriting looked like. I hope that hasn't changed *en route* here." Patrick slapped his colleague's shoulder. "Although you won't need to be any less brave than when you were facing terrorists or insurgents. Over the top it is."

Deep Under Turfy Grass

Finding an excuse to see Rafe again wasn't difficult, given that Neville had the bag of Billy's effects ready for despatch, although where they'd been hidden remained a mystery. Billy himself had known nothing about their whereabouts. Sending Patrick, in person, to ensure their safe delivery turned out to be a master stroke.

Rafe's ground floor flat was several stops west down the District line, in an area which was pleasant without being posh, and its understated decor, seen through the bay window, spoke of taste and class. He answered the door promptly, greeting his guest with a wistful smile. Patrick accepted the offer of coffee and the chance to talk, wondering all the time what Christopher would have done if he had been sent to do this. What he was doing, now, if he was supposed to have Rafe's interest in his charge.

"I'm grateful. It may not seem much to you, but this means all the world to me." Rafe fingered the parcel. "Once I've got these put away then I feel I can say goodbye. Properly."

Patrick nodded, but he didn't produce a platitude. When people said, "I know how you feel," it usually meant they didn't. "It may not help, but I was asked to pass on the gratitude of the woman whose daughter Billy saved from the lorry. She says she'll never forget his courage."

Rafe shook his head. "Typical bloody thing he'd have done. Please don't," he said, shooting Patrick a warning glance, "give me any crap about his dying a heroic death. I think I'd rather it had just been an accident."

How bloody ironic. Patrick held his tongue; what would have been the use of trying to reassure Rafe now?

"I'm an ungrateful sod, I know, but I can't help wishing he'd have put himself—or me—first, for once." Rafe wiped his eye, whether from a tear or a speck of dust he wasn't making plain. "Always had to do his duty, my Billy. Whatever the cost."

"I never met him before he died," Patrick felt he had to tell the literal truth, "but that equates with everything I've heard."

"People tell me I should start to get out more, maybe try and meet someone else. I'm not sure I want to."

"You told me about a mate of yours you went to the rugby with..."

"Robbie? Yeah, he's a good sort. Made my life the nearest thing it could be to bearable the last few months." Rafe eyed the package again.

This was surely the moment to settle the deal, with him at his most vulnerable? "I've something else for you, too." Patrick reached into the inside pocket of his jacket. "Billy wrote this but didn't get the chance to post it. It's addressed to you."

Rafe took the envelope with shaking hands. "Why didn't I get this before?"

"Beats me. Lost in transit?" Patrick tried to sound convincing, although Rafe was so intent on looking at Billy's handwriting that it was unlikely he'd notice one way or the other. "You've got it now. That's all that matters." He put down his mug. "I'd better go, so you can read that in private."

"No, there's no need. I've waited long enough, it'll keep a while longer." Rafe smiled. "Finish your coffee. You deserve it. I just wish I could show my gratitude a bit more effectively."

Patrick swallowed hard. Those words, that phrasing— he was back a hundred years and sitting on a garden seat with Christopher. The memory of ensuing events produced a blush, vivid enough to have to disguise; thank goodness for the large mug of coffee to hand.

"It's my pleasure," he said, when he finally felt able to speak again. "I could say it was all part of the job, but it's been more than that. This time."

Rafe nodded. "Yes, I think I can understand that." Although what he understood Patrick wasn't sure and didn't want to ask.

The Last Laugh

Billy stood outside the pub, doing what Rafe would have called dithering, something which—in the past—would only have showed up in civvy street and never when on operations. *Don't lose your touch now*. He took a deep breath and was about to go in when he felt a slap in the small of his back.

"Nice to see you here again."

Billy span round, afraid he'd been confronted by someone who used to know him, but it was only Simon Youngs, clearly *en route* for his usual place at the bar. "Hi. Yep. Bad penny, always coming around."

"Billy Byrne used to say something like that." Simon grinned.

Damn. He'd have to be more careful, although Simon didn't seemed to have noticed.

"It's Wednesday, so Robbie should be here. Remember that bloke I told you about?"

"Oh, yeah. I'd like to meet him."

"If he's not here already, hang around. He's bound to swing by." Simon took Billy's arm and nudged him towards the door. "Fancy a drink while we wait?"

"I wouldn't say no to a pint." And a double whisky chaser, the way his stomach was churning.

The beer had to wait. The shortest route from door to bar had Robbie Woodward, deep in conversation with another bloke, right in the middle of it. Simon's primary way of making contact was clearly slapping people in the middle of their backs and winding them. He used it now.

Robbie almost spilled his pint, although he didn't lose his rag, grinning and saying, "Simon. Can you not stop bouncing around like a puppy? And who's this you've got in tow?" He gave Billy a smile.

"This is Robin." Simon clearly thought that was enough of an introduction. "I'll be at the bar."

"Were you looking for me? Simon seems to think we have stuff to talk about."

Billy wasn't going to admit that maybe he'd misjudged Robbie—the short time at HQ hadn't mellowed him that much, and the old feelings took over pretty damn quick back here—but if Rafe liked him then perhaps he wasn't quite as bad as his jealousy had made out. He was almost handsome, from the right angle, and evidently popular. "Yeah. I was hoping to run into you, it being Wednesday."

"Simon knows I'm a creature of habit." Robbie leaned a couple of inches closer, narrowing his eyes in a shrewd appreciation of the man addressing him. "Do I know you?"

"We may have run across each other, I'm not sure. Someone seems to have mixed us up, though." Billy slipped his hand into his inside pocket. "My name's Robin Woodfall. Some idiot of a postman tried to deliver this to me." He produced an envelope—what any soldier would have recognised as official forces post, a "bluey"—with Robbie Woodward's name and address scrawled on it with just enough illegibility to have confused some half—awake postal employee.

"I can see why they got mixed up with the name, but don't tell me you live in the same road?" Robbie looked sceptical; he clearly wouldn't take even Neville's forgery boys' expert counterfeit of postmarks and redirections at face value.

"I don't. I'm in Whitemill Avenue, about three roads down from you." Billy tried a reassuring smile. "Not as posh as Whitemill Lane, but we're always getting your post. And pizza deliveries." He held out the letter again. "It's not mine and if it's not yours I've no idea where to take the bloody thing."

Robbie took the envelope, turning pale when he got a good look at the handwriting. "Looks like they've misread the house number first time around. How did you work out it could be mine?"

"I'm not psychic, if that's what you're thinking. It had already been redirected when it came to me—they must cover the two roads from the same sorting office. I opened the bloody envelope without thinking." Billy pointed at the tape used to reseal it; this was a meticulous piece of forgery. "Whoever wrote this was brought up to do things properly. There's an address inside and enough of the name to work it out. I'm just sorry it took so long." Billy tried to pre—empt any question about the time lag. "I've been away on business, so this has been gathering dust on my desk, just where my cleaner left it."

It looked like Robbie was beginning to believe what he'd been told. "I'm grateful, I think." He eyed the envelope again. "If this is from who I think it's from, then maybe I won't be, when I've read it." He gave Billy a sharp look. "Have *you* read it?"

"I couldn't help seeing the first couple of lines, but I soon realised it was personal."

How easy it had become to play ignorance. Billy knew every word of that letter by heart, which of course he would, having written it. A message from beyond the grave about letting bygones be bygones and asking, if anything happened to him, for Robbie to keep an eye on Rafe. It didn't actually say, "I give you my permission to bed him," although anyone with any sense would read between the lines and find a blessing on a future relationship.

"Can I get you a drink? You've gone to a lot of trouble."

"I wouldn't say no to a pint." Billy's mouth felt dry as the deserts he'd operated in.

"Pint it is. Excuse us," Robbie said to his friends, turning to lead the way to the bar. "I'm still not clear how you found me." He didn't sound accusatory, simply perplexed.

"Lucky coincidence. I happened to be here talking to Simon and his mates, and you got mentioned. From the little information I had, I put two and two together. Lucky I got four and not five."

"Lucky coincidences happen." Robbie waved a tenner at the barman. "Maybe someone up there's looking after us."

Billy wasn't going to argue.

Smile, Smile, Smile

The snow had thawed at last, almost as suddenly as it had come, according to Neville, and the blue of the sky spoke of warmer days just around the corner. Patrick was reading the newspaper, still affronted that the war to end all wars had failed so dismally at ending any of them. Familiar places—even if some of the names had changed—were still being torn apart. He looked up as the door opened and a handsome face, not unlike Rafe Whittaker's, appeared around it.

"I'm looking for Patrick." The new arrival scanned the room, even though there was only one occupant.

"You've found him." Patrick vaulted from his chair, holding out a hand to be shaken. "Pleased to meet you. It's been too quiet here—nice to see a new face."

"The face may be new, but the person behind it isn't." The newcomer smiled, smoothing back his hair in a characteristic gesture Patrick hadn't seen in a century. "Hello, Paddy."

Patrick's heart leaped. "Christopher?"

"The same." The tentative handshake turned into a spontaneous embrace, warmer even than the sunshine which was hard at work melting the last of the ice outside. "I should have known you straight away. I'm sorry."

"My own mother wouldn't recognise me." Patrick let the embrace go on as long as was decent, not that he thought Neville would mind. It was surely no coincidence that they had the house practically to themselves. He sat down again, legs suddenly unsteady. "You look...familiar."

"And so I should." Christopher grabbed a small chair, turning it around in order to straddle it, just as he used to all those years ago. "You've done the business for young Rafe?"

Patrick nodded, sitting upright with his hands between his knees, still a bit awkward. Like they were back to those first, hesitant, unsure days of courtship. "Our part of the job's done. Billy gave Robbie 'the talk' and we believe there's already been action taken. *Orders is orders*. You can do your bit now."

"Aye." Christopher seemed thoughtful. "What did you make of Rafe?"

"Nice bloke. I'm not sure he doesn't deserve something better than Robbie but..." Patrick shrugged, still smiling. "Someone thinks they need to be together. Any idea why?"

"Yes." Christopher stood, turned the chair its proper way round, then sat again. The same sign he'd always used that the discussion was about to become serious. He didn't elaborate further at this point about what he meant. That habit hadn't changed in all this time, either.

Patrick didn't hurry to press him for an answer; to be in the same room again, together, was a pleasure to be savoured. Nowhere else felt this comfortable. "Neville said you had a vested interest in this case. Would you tell me what it is?"

Christopher smiled. A rueful, sad smile, the same one he'd worn when saying goodbye to Patrick on a cold station, back in 1916 when they'd managed to wangle their periods of leave to coincide. "He's my great—grandson."

"Your…?" Even after all that had happened the last few days, Patrick hadn't believed he could still feel so faint, experience such a kick in the teeth.

"Steady on, old man." Christopher was quickly up and at his side, arm around him. "Sorry, that must have been a hell of a shock. I was hoping somebody had told you."

"I had no idea." None at all. Did that explain all that time back at HQ, waiting for Christopher to show up and always being disappointed? For a long time he'd assumed that his lover was still alive, and when that reached the point it couldn't be true, Patrick had assumed they'd been kept apart for some reason. Not allowed to be together yet, maybe not allowed to be together ever. Perhaps they'd got it all entirely wrong and Leviticus was right, despite what the gospels said. "I didn't know what had happened to you."

"And you didn't bother to find out?" Christopher didn't seem angry—this was like his lover of old, always teasing. Maybe this wasn't his first angelic assignment and he'd got the knack of reading exactly what was going on in other people's brains. Maybe they'd just clicked again, after all this time; they'd always known what the other was thinking.

"I wasn't sure I wanted to know, back at HQ." He'd worried that there'd been an equivalent to Robbie, although he'd never expected children—and therefore women—to cross his lover's horizon.

"I'm not sure you'll want to know, now you're back here." Christopher shook his head, but he didn't loosen his grip. "I ended up married. Don't ask me why, because I'm not sure I can answer the question for myself." He laughed, his face—familiar and yet strange—even more handsome than it had been when they'd known each other before. Less careworn and troubled. "I could be glib and say that men were in short supply after the war, that the pressure from my family to do my duty and conform to expectations became too much. I could say a million things but the truth is I just didn't care anymore. If you weren't there then nothing really mattered."

"Really?" Why doubt it? Patrick could imagine himself feeling the same way had the situation been reversed.

"Of course. I could only ever love you." Christopher sighed. "Carrie was a nice girl. She wanted to get away from her family and I wanted to help out, even if we were no more than friends."

"But you had children?" It still hurt, even though it wasn't strictly infidelity. The thought of his lover enjoying intimacy with anyone else rankled.

"I gave her the child she wanted, like a nice obedient bull going to the field, and that was it, really. We lived more like brother and sister than lovers. There'd never been a lot of action in the bedroom, which suited Carrie just fine. It wouldn't have been like that with us, would it? If…"

If. How many things did that small word encompass?

"I can't imagine we'd have had the chance to find out. Had we both survived," Patrick said. What sort of life

189

could they have carved together, given the hostile attitudes of law, church and both sets of parents? Sharing a house as bachelors in their twenties they might have got away with, but the "till death us do part" bit would have taken some doing. "Did Carrie know about us?"

"I never told her, although I suppose she guessed. Your picture was always on my desk and I suspect the 'old colleague, died in the trenches' line began to wear thin. She didn't mention you, although she always made sure that picture was kept scrupulously clean. There was never a mark on the frame." Christopher took a deep breath.

Patrick guided them both onto the settee, but fought against enfolding his friend in his arms, putting up the barriers to the world as they'd done so often before, and saying to hell with Rafe and Billy and Neville and the lot of them. He was a soldier, and he had his duty to do, duty which might be made easier by his unexpected moment of illumination. "What's all this about, Christopher? Are Billy and I supposed to be making sure your Rafe doesn't do the same as you?"

"Of course. There's a woman he works with, nice enough girl, but she's biding her time, hoping to catch him when he's most vulnerable again."

"His secretary?" Patrick suddenly remembered the protective, proprietary way she'd dealt with Rafe.

"That's her. She was spitting nails when she found out that he was contemplating suicide and hadn't let her be the one whose shoulder he cried on. She won't let him slip through her clutches next time." Christopher's smile lit the room again. "But there won't be a next time now,

not with that scallywag Robbie to keep an eye on things."
He gave Patrick a squeeze. "I'm glad they gave you two
the job—I'd have made a mess of it. Too close to home."

"It felt pretty close to home for us, too." Patrick
returned the smile.

"So I heard. Still, now you've sorted that part of it we
can get on with the real task in hand."

Real task? Didn't they give old soldiers a break any
more? "Which is?"

"Making sure Rafe does what he's best suited for. His
talents are completely wasted in securitisation."

"I'll pretend I know what that means." Patrick wound
his arm around his friend's shoulder, caressing the back of
his neck and the gentle curve up to his ears. He wasn't
sure if angels were allowed to kiss, once they were back
on earth, although he was pretty certain they'd be finding
out within the next ten minutes. If it meant incurring the
wrath of Neville, so be it.

"It's not important. What does matter is that there's
an opportunity going to be coming up soon. Or, at least,
we have to make sure that it does." Christopher grinned,
leaning into the embrace. "I'd forgotten how distracting
you were."

"Want me to leave off?" Patrick knew what the
answer would be.

"Of course not, you silly sod."

"Are you too distracted to tell me about this
opportunity?" At least setting that up didn't sound like it
would tug at anyone's heartstrings.

"Not yet. It's for a charitable trust that needs someone to properly handle the legal side of things."

"And presumably they don't have that already? Is someone taking advantage of them?" Patrick tried to keep one step ahead—he wasn't going to get tripped up on this mission.

"They do and yes. But not from outside."

"You must be distracted. That makes no sense," Patrick said, removing his hand from Christopher's left ear. "No more tickling until you've briefed me properly."

"Spoilsport." Christopher pointed to the briefcase he'd left by the table. "The background's all in there so you can research to your heart's content. Cut short, the present occupant of the post is starting to be, let's say, a little too free and easy with where the money's actually going."

"Into his own pocket, I presume?" The temptation to rub his friend's neck—that beautifully fluffy skin—was strong, but Patrick resisted.

"Eventually, yes. But it's cleverly done and it'll be the Dickens to prove so we'll have our work cut out. I can foresee lots of nudging people in the right direction to accumulate the evidence and then act before he causes too much devastation."

"One of those key points in the process control system?"

"You've been talking to Neville," Christopher said, tipping his head to one side like he always did when amused. As Rafe had done. "Yes. It may seem small beer now, but down the line the effects could be huge."

"And once we've sorted that side, we make sure Rafe gets nudged into applying?"

Christopher nodded. "He'll be happier by then, with Robbie close at hand. His head will have got to the right place for taking a few risks. In five years' time, if the right flowchart pathways get followed, he'll be leading the trust, so long as we keep any obstacles out of his path. There's a few on the way that we may have to come back and help him divert."

"You keep saying we. Is Billy helping as well?"

"You never were the brightest candle on the candelabra, were you?" Christopher rubbed his knuckles on his old friend's head, just as he'd done when they were first lovers, and hardly more than boys. "Billy's on the periphery of this one, as he'll have much more important things to be dealing with. Just you and me, Paddy boy. This is our operation."

Back here on earth, pain, doubt and frustration had returned, made worse to endure by all the time at HQ where they'd been nothing but a vague memory. Even so, Patrick hadn't anticipated that when joy came back it would feel so much more intense than it had a hundred years before. "Working together? That's wonderful."

"Neville can be inspired at times. He thinks we could be the perfect team for this."

Perfect team. That's what they'd always thought of themselves. But if that was the case, why hadn't they met up at HQ? The cold reality of that simple fact hit Patrick in the guts like a fist blow. "Why didn't you try to find me?

Back at HQ. Was it because of Carrie, that they wouldn't allow us to meet again?"

"Carrie? Don't you remember that men and women don't marry in heaven?" Christopher pulled his old lover towards him, cradling Patrick's head under his chin. "I had the same doubts, especially after I got there and didn't find you waiting for me, champagne bottle in hand. I asked Marjorie about it."

"And she said?" Patrick snuggled into the comforting embrace.

"She said I had to be patient. 'There are many rooms in our Father's house and many jobs to do, young man'." It was easy to see where Rafe had got his gift for impersonations. "I'm glad we met back here, though."

Patrick felt like an hour had passed before he could dare speak. Even then he couldn't have the guts to say what he really meant, not yet. Maybe there'd be many more of these missions to undertake and they could share the time—and perhaps themselves? HQ was wonderful, beyond all imagining, but a cuddle on a sofa, with the thought of more to come, wasn't half bad. "I guess we had to put some things right for other people before we could have ourselves put right." It sounded even more banal spoken than thought, but that simple phrase hid a wealth of emotion.

"Something like that, I guess." Christopher kissed the top of Patrick's head. "And at least now we'll always have world enough and time."

"Yes." They used up a good portion of time just sitting and holding each other, listening to the birds outside and the steady breathing inside. "The answer will be in that briefcase but I'll ask anyway. What's the charitable trust for? The one we want Rafe to take over."

"Can't you guess? Old soldiers, Paddy boy. Old soldiers."